W9-CKM-751

The Family Lie

GEORGES SIMENON

The Family Lie

Translated by Isabel Quigly

A Helen and Kurt Wolff Book

Harcourt Brace Jovanovich

New York and London

Copyright 1940 by Librairie Gallimard
English translation copyright © 1978 by Georges Simenon

All rights reserved. No part of this publication may
be reproduced or transmitted in any form or by any means,
electronic or mechanical, including photocopy, recording,
or any information storage and retrieval system,
without permission in writing from the publisher.

Printed in the United States of America

Library of Congress Cataloging in Publication Data
Simenon, Georges, 1903–
The family lie.

Translation of Malempin.
"A Helen and Kurt Wolff book."
I. Title.
PZ3.S5892Fam   843′ .9′12   78–53898
ISBN 0–15–156247–4

First American edition

B C D E

The Family Lie

1

Even considering it coolly, I still feel that that particular day went by rather faster than usual, and the word *dizzy* comes naturally to mind. Somewhere in the depths of my memory I have an old recollection rather like it. I was playing in the schoolyard. No, I can't have been, because a streetcar comes into it. Never mind! In a street. Or a square. More likely in a square, because I can see trees and can say quite definitely that they were standing out against a white wall. I was running. Running till I was out of breath. Why? I've forgotten. I was running as you do in a dream, seeing nothing, the ground flying away under my feet like a railway embankment. And suddenly, although I was already going abnormally fast, I ran even faster, in a crescendo of speed that ended in a sudden stop which left me shaking from head to foot, temples throbbing, lips wet, eyes wide open, in front of a streetcar that, a yard away, was also shaking, all the way down the rails.

I'm not trying to prove anything. Is it that I was running

faster, on that particular day, because I had an intuition, because I could sense some catastrophe?

"Idiot!" the conductor yelled at me, as pale as I was.

I had to step back to the sidewalk. Then I sat down on a doorstep.

The day I want to talk about had no obvious connection with this. Unless, perhaps, a certain gaiety that scented those fine June days? I got up at six, before the maid had come down. While I was shaving in the bathroom, my wife called to me from bed:

"Don't forget the insurance. . . ."

Rue de Beaune was empty. On Quai d'Orsay I took a taxi and was driven to Saint-Lazare, across a Paris golden as a peach.

Nothing out of the ordinary about my doings or my movements: two croissants and a cup of coffee at the station buffet; newspapers that I read in the compartment, pausing now and then to look out at the countryside through the window.

At Evreux, Fachot met me at the station with his small car. Now there's a man it's good to see. The saints must have been like him, anxious to bring you a little joy, to spare you the smallest unpleasantness, the slightest mishap.

"My wife's got a bite ready for you."

None of this matters, but days spent with Fachot are always unlike any others. In my family, in what we call "the Malempin language," we say: "Going to the Little Sisters."

Fachot is a physician in a nursing home—or, more precisely, a hospital—run by the Little Sisters of the Poor. Many of the nuns have consumption. Fachot, who is only slightly younger than I am but hasn't quite enough self-confidence, calls for my assistance from time to time, once a month or every couple of months, to remove stitches, or sometimes for a pneumothorax.

Why are they always gay, sunny days, days of memorable sweetness? First of all, because of Fachot and his wife, of course, and the charming house they live in, right out in the country, very close to the convent. Then because of the Little Sisters, for whom it is all a party and who prepare touching surprises for me.

From nine in the morning till midday, that time, I removed the stitches of three patients, one of whom I had been looking after for several years and who always asked about my children as if she knew them. So much so that Jean and Bilot had become like members of her own family; she even slipped a bar of chocolate into my pocket.

At lunch, I told Fachot:

"Tomorrow morning we're leaving for the South. . . ."

It was the first time such a thing had happened to us. As a rule we spend our holidays near Concarneau, at Beuzec-Conq, where we have a small house. But this wasn't yet vacation time. It had taken a whole series of chances to bring about this trip.

First, Bilot's measles. He had been free of them for only the last two days and was still pretty weak. Because of the infection, his brother hadn't been to school for the past weeks.

After that, one week more or less . . .

Finally, I'd bought a new car. I'd be getting it right away. To Fachot I explained:

"We're setting off, quite haphazardly, without making any plans. . . . Orange, Avignon, Arles, Nîmes . . . My wife doesn't know the South. . . . Nor do the children . . ."

Neither did Fachot, poor soul, who was consumptive himself and would have been more at home in the mountains. I was almost ashamed of my joy.

The train . . . A taxi to get to Quai de Javel . . . It was ten past two. . . . An hour spent anxiously in the showroom where dozens of new cars were waiting, and signing forms in office after office.

At last I had the too flashy car, which was too much like a new toy. What was it my wife had reminded me of? Insurance . . . But first of all I wanted a luggage rack like the one I'd seen on a car belonging to one of the interns. The minutes were beginning to matter. I drove along Avenue de la Grande-Armée, and, being unused to the new car, scraped one of the fenders. What did it matter?

I wasn't a schoolboy on the day before vacation, yet I'm sure the blood was running faster through my veins. My cheeks were slightly flushed, as happens to me sometimes. I kept thinking about the insurance.

But first, I had to drop in on my mother. I drove along Rue Championnet. As usual, I raised my head and glanced up at the fourth-floor windows. They were closed, but my mother had seen me. Always, when I reached the fourth floor—there's no elevator—my mother had already opened the door.

"Funny color for a doctor!" she grumbled, shutting the door behind her.

It took me a moment to realize she was talking about the green color of the car. My other cars had been black. I'd I'd always wanted a green one.

"Did you sell the old one?"

"I traded it in."

"For how much? Guillaume would have paid you the same price, in installments."

The sideboard was there in the gloom, with its set of Marans stoneware. It's the only good piece of furniture in the place, the one thing I long to inherit. But I know perfectly well that Guillaume will get it, if only to spite me.

"Did he come today?"

"He had lunch with me."

Guillaume is always welcome at my mother's, whose savings he has got his hands on. And when, in her turn, she gets a little money out of me, it's to hand it on to him. What was my brother's last job? Something like manager of a small, not very reputable theater.

"Is it all arranged? You're off to the South?"

"Tomorrow . . ."

"I can think of people who need it more. . . ."

Hell, my brother, Guillaume! His wife, who's a chronic invalid, and his son, who is retarded. They live in the suburbs, near Courbevoie, because the air's healthy, they say.

"You're in a hurry?"

"Well, I've got to take care of the insurance and go to the hospital. . . ."

"Don't be late because of me!"

It's true, I never know how to take my leave. I dawdled in that apartment that smelled of solitary old women.

"I thought you were in a rush?"

"Well, good-by then, Mother . . . See you in a couple of weeks."

Even the staircase of that house gave me a sinking feeling. Was there anything I'd forgotten? Oh, yes, my little patient in bed. I'd promised her a doll. With the one-way traffic it was a problem stopping outside a shop, but I didn't have time to run around the big stores. I chose a doll dressed in blue, then crossed the Seine. I must really ask a mechanic, I thought, if the throbbing I could hear under the hood was quite normal. I drove into the hospital courtyard and knew the doorman would come and have a look at the car.

"Everything in order, Mademoiselle Berthe?"

"I'd like you to have a look at number seven, doctor."

Quick, my white coat! I shook hands with a colleague, who called:

"Tomorrow, then?"

I'd talked about it, perhaps a bit too much. What was it I had forgotten? Not the right moment to worry about that. Mademoiselle Berthe dragged me from ward to ward, from bed to bed.

"Would you go and get the doll from my car?"

I realized she wouldn't recognize my new car, and called her back.

"The green one!"

And I sat down on my small patient's bed, Number 11. Would she still be here two weeks from now? It seemed as if she could read my thoughts.

"Will you be away long, doctor?"

"A week or two . . ."

She looked very sad. I knew why and didn't dare mention it. She was thirteen and understood everything.

"I do wish you could be here."

She barely glanced at the doll, just enough to make me think she was pleased. She was, too. The nurse waited, annoyed.

I was still expected at the outpatient clinic. The intern had already started consultations. It was somewhat chaotic, with people who'd talk about their illnesses for hours if you'd listen, watching you suspiciously.

The insurance! I'd nearly forgotten it, and the old police station had closed down last week. What time did the offices in Rue Le Peletier close?

"Good-by, doctor! Have a nice vacation. . . ."

Why had I been hounded since morning by a haste that hadn't gained me a second? What was I afraid of? For a moment I had a feeling that I was trying to escape something, to cheat fate.

The thermos bottles! I'd promised Jeanne to bring two thermos bottles, so that we need not go to a restaurant and could have lunch beside the road. There was a shop opposite Montparnasse station. It was the nearest. A policeman made me repark the car, because it was facing the wrong way.

A hundred and twenty francs each, but they were covered with real leather. As the salesman put it, they'd last a life-time.

It was too late to go to Rue Le Peletier. The offices were closed. I'd send a check with all the necessary information tonight.

Should I take the car to a garage? Better leave it in our street. Jean would want to admire it. I honked briefly three times, as I used to with the old one, but they couldn't have recognized the new horn.

The elevator. My hand in my pocket, groping for the key. I frowned to see the door open, as happened with my mother but never here. It wasn't even the maid who'd done it. It was my wife. She wasn't out of control—she never is—

but her features were more drawn than usual, her lips dry, her eyes sunken.

"Bilot," she murmured, grabbing my hat and bag.

Why did I guess? I went straight to Bilot's room, where he ought not to have been at that hour. The apartment was dark, because the day wasn't quite over and the children's room was the only one with a light on. Bilot was in bed, very pale, his mouth open, breathing with difficulty.

My legs trembled for a moment, as they had in front of the streetcar, and I looked straight ahead of me, unable to pull myself together.

"At four o'clock, he was running a temperature of a hundred and three," murmured my wife, who had come noiselessly in. "I've sent Jean to the Courdercs. . . ."

She thought of everything. She stayed calm and deliberate, as if this were a way to fend off trouble.

"Call Morin," I said. "Tell him to come at once. If he isn't at home, get them to call the nursing home."

Not a word about the illness, but I knew we both had the same thought.

Jean, the elder, who's eleven, has been growing up without trouble, without ailments or accidents. It's almost a shock to see him, broad and ruddy and bursting with health, beside pale, gentle Bilot, whose eight years have been dogged by every possible illness and the stupidest of accidents.

So much so that I was amazed, several days ago, to see his measles over without complications. Astonished and worried, I must admit.

It wasn't the reason for my haste throughout the day, but I'm sure there was some nagging unease.

Why did I think of diphtheria, even before I bent over him? It has always frightened us, Jeanne and me. Is it because Bilot has had tonsillitis every year?

But I'd seen a case the previous week, at the hospital, in the bed next to Number 11, whom I'd moved. A little boy of four, who'd died under Béraud.

"Morin's on his way," my wife told me.

And I said softly:

"Jean mustn't come home for supper. Couldn't he stay with the Courdercs?"

"I don't feel I can ask them. Shall I take him to your mother's?"

There was already something stifling about the apartment, and the light seemed to have dimmed.

"We must get some serum ready. . . ."

"Thirty cubic centimeters?" asked Jeanne.

I understood when I saw my medical textbook, open at the page for diphtheria, on the children's desk. She had read it. Yet she kept calm.

"There's the bell. It must be Morin."

"You'd better leave us. Look after Jean, while he's here. Take the car and drive him to my mother's. . . ."

Morin was cool and precise. His silvery hair gave him a stern appearance, yet he didn't frighten children. Like any other parent of a sick child, I explained:

"I've been away since this morning. . . . When I got back . . ."

"Open your mouth, son. . . . Don't be frightened. . . . Pass me the tongue depressor, Malempin."

Gentle Bilot puts up with illness uncomplainingly. Why was I looking at the page of my medical text? I knew what it said. I may not be a specialist in children's diseases, like Morin, but . . .

Well! I was wrong a little earlier. The sudden stop, with sweat on my upper lip, a thundering in my head, a sudden weakening of my legs, the arrest corresponding to that at the streetcar—all that struck me now. I read: "malignant diphtheria." Then farther on, the word *Marfan.*

Marfan diphtheria.

When I was astounded that the child in the hospital had died, in spite of powerful doses of serum, Béraud told me about Marfan diphtheria, which is rare.

And now I no longer dared turn to the bed, to Morin. I was sure that was it. I was sure that Bilot wouldn't even be lucky enough to get ordinary diphtheria. Hadn't he always picked up unusual illnesses?

"There is suprarenal insufficiency, as well as debility and low blood pressure, but the serious symptoms as a rule appear about the tenth day, brutally, resulting in sudden death, accompanied by extreme pallor . . ."

Morin was doing his job conscientiously, as I had done mine earlier at the hospital. He took a little whitish matter from Bilot's throat.

"We must get some serum ready," he told me, stuffing a glass tube with cotton. "Will you take care of it?"

"I'd rather . . ."

"Right . . . Are you keeping him here?"

I looked down. He understood. I explained:

"I've had the elder boy taken to my mother's. . . ."

I have rarely heard the sounds of Paris so intensely, and up to midnight I was startled every three minutes when a bus stopped quite close to our street door.

"What did he say?" I had asked my wife when she returned.

"He didn't want to sleep at your mother's, because he doesn't like the musty smell there."

Did we eat? I know I went into the kitchen. I looked at the maid, who was new, and can't have been twenty, and wondered if it might not be wiser to . . . Oh, no! There were limits, even to bad luck.

Morin came back. Forty cubic centimeters, the first time; then more, an hour later.

"I think it would be best to inoculate his brother. Where is he?"

"My wife will take you. The other side of Paris."

And, to Jeanne:

"The car is still out in the street?"

There's nothing like such questions to bring you back to reality. Everything else is out of focus. When I was alone with Bilot . . .

"May I go up to bed, sir?"

The maid. Of course, of course.

There was emptiness around the two of us, then. Had I a fever, too?

Had I, like Bilot, a damp bandage around my neck that gave me a swollen feeling?

I could hear his difficult breathing; I waited for the gaps in it. And there was steam, because water had been put to boil on a stove, to keep the air moist. The mirror above the fireplace was covered with it, as it is when one has a bath. The walls were dripping, losing their substance, becoming as soft as the mattress, and weird patterns emerged from the wallpaper and the toile de Jouy curtains.

I don't think I sat down. I'd put my watch on the bed-side table. In an hour, I must give him a third serum injection, intravenously this time. And, if his throat still gave him trouble, telephone Morin to come quickly and insert a tube. The instruments were ready on a napkin.

All this I knew. These were facts, obviously. But at the same time they might be distorted by fever.

What I saw—I was standing at the foot of the bed—were Bilot's open eyes. He isn't named Bilot. It isn't a name at all. But we can hardly remember that his name is Jérôme, like his great-grandfather, because his grandmother wanted it.

It was his brother who called him "Bilot," when he was small. We never knew why; it was just that those syllables came to him.

Bilot was looking at me. Of course he's never had much color, but he had never been so pale as he was that day, and the pallor was made even more terrifying by the fever. His fair hair, so fair it looked thin, was stuck to his round forehead with sweat. The damp bandage raised his chin. He opened his small mouth like a fish. . . .

And yet he was horribly calm. He wasn't afraid. He looked at me. If I moved, however little, he followed me with his eyes.

All at once, for no reason, I turned my head away. It was absurd. I could perfectly well look at him. I tried to smile encouragingly at him.

The walls receded farther and became less solid, like everything else, furniture, objects, even the light, which no longer came from anywhere. I heard his breathing, with the inevitable impediment in the throat, the rattle that wasn't quite one but that almost stopped me from breathing freely as well.

Jeanne must have arrived at my mother's, and she—my mother—must have been delighted. If Jeanne didn't stop her, she'd want Jean to sleep in her bed. But Jeanne would never allow it.

Bilot looked at me. . . . How long had he been looking at me like that, gravely? I write "gravely" because I can't find another word. . . . It isn't curiously, either. . . . He was looking at me serenely, as if he was seeing me truly, *definitively*.

I know what I'm saying. I've changed my appearance many times. I shall change again. But Bilot, at that time, saw me definitively.

It hardly mattered what I was yesterday, and what I'd be tomorrow. I wouldn't change again. He would see me always as I was at that moment before him, and later, until I died, I would still exist in my present form.

This is what I've just discovered, and I have proof of it. My father, who died twenty-five years ago, wasn't always the same man. Yet, once, when I was about six or seven (Bilot is eight), I woke up in the middle of the night, surprised by a light. It was the light of an oil lamp. There were exposed beams above my bed, and the walls were whitewashed with lime. We lived on a farm.

My father was standing with rain dripping off him, wearing some oilskin garment. He was large, enormous, more powerful than anyone I'd ever seen; his cheeks were full and sunburned, his blue eyes slightly protuberant.

He was looking at me. Was I ill myself? Had I a fever? I don't remember having seen my mother in the room.

But I remember my father. I saw him. I heard him. He lived. He was there, just as he was, just as he had always been, just as he would always be.

And today, I . . .

Clumsily I turned, as carefully as if I were afraid of scaring a ghost. I know that Bilot's eyes were following me all the time. I would have to go to the far end of the room for him to lose sight of me, but the mirror was in the middle, above the fireplace.

Because of the steam, at first all I could make out were blurred outlines, and I had to try hard to overcome a kind of shyness in order to take a handkerchief out of my pocket and wipe the glass.

There! That was I! The proof that there was something definite in my image, that was what surprised me.

Was I expecting to see a small boy or an adolescent?

How, almost without my noticing it, had I managed to become nearly as big as my father? I was big, too. In bulk, about the same, but my father was hard and my outlines had something soft about them. Above all, there was something I didn't like—swellings on my face, particularly on the sides of my nose.

I was wearing a blue suit. I had forgotten it. I was fat, that was obvious, and beginning to show a paunch.

It was I! There was no doubt about it. That was what Bilot was looking at and *that* would no longer change.

What was he thinking as he saw me in front of the mirror? I didn't dare turn toward him. He ought to have looked at me earlier, when I was less paunchy, less soft, but he was then too young.

He trusted me. I was sure he had complete trust in me, very different from that which he had in his mother. He wasn't afraid of his illness. He wasn't afraid of dying.

I was there!

I ought to have turned to the bedside table to check the time on my watch, but I kept putting it off. There were several minutes to go before the third injection. Better for my wife to be there. She must have been worried about settling Jean in and frightened at the idea of infection. . . . It's Jean who matters most to her.

As for me . . . No! I have no reason to love my elder boy any less than Bilot. Is it because Bilot notices that I have bags under my eyes? And that in the lower part of my face there's a puffiness that makes it look weak? Yes, that's it. I seem weak. I seem powerless. And he trusts me! To him, I am a man—that is, a complete solid being on whom he can lean.

"It doesn't hurt too much?"

Why did I speak? To give myself the excuse of looking at him. He couldn't answer, but his eyes moved. You'd swear he was trying to reassure me.

Later, if he . . . I touched wood, in spite of myself. Later, he'll probably say to himself, wonderingly:

"Was my father . . ."

Was my father really like that? And what will he base it on, since I shall no longer be there? Will he question the survivors? Perhaps my wife, because I'm sure that in spite of her poor health she'll live to be very old, just like my mother.

Another ten minutes. By then, Jeanne would be back. If a tube was needed . . .

He kept watching me, all the time. His eyes were shining and slightly puzzled, but they never left me. Was he thinking? Or did the fever leave nothing in his head but a chaos of jumbled images?

The night I looked at my father . . . And suddenly I was ashamed, feeling I'd been unfair. Ever since then, since I was seven, I'd been satisfied with that one image of my father.

I'd never tried to know. Worse! I must be really honest: I'd never wanted to know.

For years and years, I preferred not to think about it. I almost used guile in order to avoid thinking about it. I hastened to accept what happened: my father buried in Saint-Jean-d'Angély, my mother settled for her old age on Rue Championnet, my brother and . . .

Yet one night, one rainy winter's night, my father had stood by my bed and watched me. He had lighted the lamp in order to watch me. He was grave.

I was sure, now, suddenly, that he was more than grave. And I was sure that it was connected with all that had happened before, with all that happened later and that I didn't want to know.

They told me:

"Your uncle Tesson has disappeared. . . ."

They told me:

"Your aunt is a bitch. . . ."

They told me:

"She'd sooner leave her money to charity. . . ."

And I took no notice of anything. When, in Paris, I got the telegram announcing my father's death, I arrived just in time for a look at him before they nailed down the coffin lid, and it isn't only what he looked like then that I don't remember. I went to the funeral and all I remember is the cold in my feet and hands.

"It's you!" I said, realizing my voice sounded odd.

It was my wife, who'd just come in and wasn't really looking at me. I now had a wife and children!

"You've forgotten to fill it up again," she said, going across to the saucepan, which was nearly empty.

"Yes . . . my head's swimming." Mechanically I raised Bilot's wrist to take his pulse and forgot to count.

"Have you got the serum?"

Bilot hadn't looked at her. He was taken up entirely with me. He let me uncover him, inject into the vein.

"We mustn't forget to tell them at the town hall. . . ."

I could no longer follow, but it didn't matter. Or, rather, it did. I came back. We had to declare a contagious disease.

Now that Jeanne was there, I fell back into ordinary life and it didn't seem very real to me—which was strange.

Had I really lived for forty-two years and . . .

"Turn over, dear. . . . Don't be afraid. . . ."

He wasn't afraid. Was I afraid of my father? Is anyone afraid of a man?

At five in the morning, we had to call Morin to insert a tube. Could it be otherwise? Must not poor Bilot expect the worst, as always?

The book had stayed open on the table, beside a children's notebook: ". . . but the serious symptoms as a rule appear about the tenth day, brutally . . ."

"Haven't you called the hospital?" Jeanne asked me, toward morning.

Why, since I was on vacation? No one except Morin and my mother knew I was in Paris.

With the help of the maid, whom I'd had vaccinated, to be on the safe side, I put a couch in the children's room.

I no longer knew what time it was—Jeanne had gone to see Jean at my mother's—when I laid the notebook, which had only the first page used, for an arithmetic problem, on my lap.

I had just decided to relive the moment when I opened my eyes, in my room on the farm, and saw my father, lighted by the oil lamp.

What helped me was the fact that it wasn't an ordinary winter. It was the winter when, in the whole district, from Rochefort to Saint-Jean-d'Angély, the fields were under water.

2

It wasn't raining. After thirty-five years, I can still say that for certain because the question of deciding whether to let the top down or keep it up was the object of discussion and, of course, of a quarrel.

They quarreled every Sunday; and particularly on the Sundays when we visited the Tessons. And that Sunday was one of them.

I cannot remember the date, but I suppose it was about the end of autumn, or else in the middle of a very rainy winter, because the floods, which were to worsen and become catastrophic, had already begun.

Is it because certain events impressed me violently at the time that the countryside, across the years, still has the appearance and taste of that Sunday and of the weeks that followed it? A colorless sky, with more water suspended in it; a light that came from nowhere, giving no shadows, no outline to things, accentuating the harshness of tints.

It was these tints, in fact, the tints of the surrounding countryside, that gave me nightmares, in the literal sense of the word. I was frightened by the dark green the flooded fields became in winter, icy in places where there were puddles of water with nasty little tufts of grass poking out of them; I was frightened by the trees that stood out against the sky and, above all, I don't know why, by the pollarded willows. As for the newly turned earth, the brown of it turned my stomach.

On Sunday, especially, I had the appalling feeling of an empty universe in which my small legs dared not venture, and it was with the greatest difficulty that they managed to get me out of the house.

The village was far away, at the end of a muddy road, with slimy ruts and hedges that had a nasty look about them, too, in winter. When we had passed the first bend in the road we saw a slate-covered belfry and the gable end of the first house, which had, in monstrous letters on a red background, the name of an apéritif written on it.

In the morning, we all dressed for mass, but took our Sunday clothes off right after it, since we didn't wear our good clothes at home. You could hear the cows moving about in the shed, directly beyond the kitchen wall.

Only my sister, who went to a convent boarding school in La Rochelle, and was at home on that day, kept her Sunday clothes on the whole time.

Did I ever see her wearing clogs? I don't think so. At twelve she was a young lady, thin, pale, distinguished look-ing, and it seemed as if everyone was scared of hurting her.

Another detail comes back to me suddenly and may ex-plain the tone of the Sunday arguments: at the midday meal, my father's breath smelled of alcohol. If I were to mention this to my mother, she'd deny it, but I'd swear that my memory of it is right. After mass, didn't he hang about the village for a while with the men?

We ate quickly, cleared the table even faster, and did no washing up. First my brother, Guillaume, who was only four, was dressed, and had to be kept quiet afterward so that he wouldn't get dirty again. I would hear my mother coming and going in her room, the door of which was open, calling to my sister to come and hook up her bodice.

Everyone seemed impatient, and I still wonder why. Yes, come to think of it, why were they arguing? About a match my father had thrown on the floor. About nothing. Less than nothing. And my mother's bodice wouldn't hook up. There was always something they searched for and couldn't find. Or my father had harnessed the mare too early, and, even though he said nothing, my mother claimed that he was growing impatient, that men were all alike. . . .

We had a trap with two very high wheels, rimmed with rubber, and bodywork of varnished wood. It was like the jaunting cars seen in the country and in towns on market days, but I'm sure I'm not mistaken in saying that ours was different. For instance, the lamps were made of copper and had beveled glass.

Eugène, the farm hand, who didn't have Sunday off when we went to Saint-Jean-d'Angély, watched us climb up one after another, my father and mother in front, my small brother on my mother's knees ("Don't rumple my dress!"), my sister and I behind, on the two seats facing each other.

Even now, I am dismayed by the merciless dreariness of our ride. The two backs, my father's black one, my mother's with a collar of marten fur on her coat, swayed in a slow rhythm on the hills when we went at walking pace, and at a faster rhythm on the flat ground when the mare trotted.

And everywhere hedges, and houses with their windows shut. Why did it make me sad to think of the people shut inside them? Sometimes young men in their Sunday best, their faces redder than usual above their white collars, at an inn doorway; or a family, hand in hand with the children, trailing along the empty road, from one village to the next, to visit relatives.

It took about an hour and a half from our house to Saint-Jean-d'Angély.

"Hand me the package, Mémée," my mother said, invariably at the same bend, to my sister, whose name was Edmée.

There were slices of bread, each with a bar of chocolate. We were made to eat them before going to the Tessons'. It seems that we ate too much and that, without this precaution, we would have appeared greedy. I can still taste the special flavor of those slices of bread and that chocolate.

"Don't go too fast, Arthur! Give them time to eat. . . ."

The houses in Saint-Jean-d'Angély were white, the streets even emptier than the country lanes. There was a sound of bells in the air. The shutters of the shops were down, except for one, which sold bikes, and which had a lemon-yellow front.

"Now try to behave yourselves, won't you, so that I won't have to be ashamed of you."

The carriage almost stopped, the horse reared, because it involved an awkward maneuver to get into Rue du

Chapître, which was very narrow. We scraped past the houses. I tried to make out faces behind the shutters. We stopped outside a fine doorway, and my father got us down, one after the other.

I don't think my sister ever spoke, not a single time, on the way. It is only now that this amazes me. At the time, it seemed quite natural to see her always silent, always fixed in her "medal-like" attitude.

That was another Malempin word, one of my mother's expressions:

"Edmée has the profile of a medal."

A final inspection of the whole family and my father lifted the knocker. The noise echoed far away across the paved courtyard, on the right side of which was a flight of four steps.

A ridiculous incident has just taken place and I am uneasy, even humiliated. I don't know what the time is because, to avoid tiring Bilot, we have left the curtains drawn across the windows. For a long time, this morning, I took no notice of the sounds in the street, of the bus's noisy stops.

Morin came. We exchanged fewer than a dozen sentences. What was the point? My wife took him into the next room. She must have questioned him in a low voice. Then she came back and prowled around me as if expecting something.

Why did her presence irritate me? Because I was already irritated before she spoke. Not exactly irritated, maybe, but nervous, impatient.

Impatient, yes. I wanted to see her go, in order to be alone with Bilot. Of course, I hadn't shaved. My shirt was open at the neck, and under my doctor's white coat I was wearing nothing but trousers, without suspenders.

"You ought to have a bath and change," she said at last.

"It's not worth it."

"Listen, Edouard, there's no point your staying in this room all day. . . . Why not go to the hospital?"

"They think I'm on the way to the South. . . ."

"You can take a vacation later on, when he's recovered. . . ."

I was annoyed. Annoyed by her presence. And, to make a clean breast of it, annoyed at seeing her interfering in men's business.

I can perfectly well work out my feelings: my father, myself, Bilot . . . I was into it up to the neck; I wasn't going to let a woman . . .

Impatiently I replied:

"Why don't you go and see *your* son!"

That meant Jean, whom for the first time I was calling *her* son.

She answered no less nervously:

"You know I don't particularly like going to *your* mother's!"

We both were sorry. When she was leaving the room, I felt she was on the point of tears. I heard her dressing in her room. Then I ran into the living room, opened the window, and saw her starting the car.

Too bad.

That Sunday, like the others, my father waited in the court-yard while we went into the hall, then, having taken off our coats, into the room on the left, where we used to sit. I had to kiss my aunt Elise's pink, scented cheeks and my uncle Tesson's tobacco-reeking face.

The windows were very high. I saw my father unharnessing the mare. In that urban courtyard, he seemed to me bigger and more powerful than ever, and as if ashamed of his height and heaviness.

He wasn't at home there. I am sure he was reluctant to come. He led the mare across the garden with great care, because once there had been complaints that she had trampled on a rosebush or a rhododendron.

The trap stayed by the door, silly and useless with its shafts sticking upward. Without hurrying, my father put a halter on the mare and fastened it to a ring in the greenhouse wall.

If he could have done so, he would probably have put off even longer the moment of entering the house, where each person took his seat, as if in the theater, and never moved.

If my father was impressed, so was I, and for a long time my idea of riches was mingled with my picture of the house in Rue du Chapître. The front steps seemed to me majestic. The hall was large, paved with blue and white flagstones, its ceiling so high that voices became strikingly loud.

Several times I managed to catch a glimpse of a room that was generally shut, on the right, with walls of pearl-gray woodwork, crimson brocade curtains, and armchairs set in a circle, as if for some majestic council, around a pink marble table.

There was also my uncle's study, which seemed to me very large. Everything was big in that house from an earlier century, even the wall telephone, which was of an old-fashioned kind, with pigeonholes and file cards next to it. And I never realized that the pervasive smell was merely one of mustiness.

"You've taken the wrong chair again," my mother scolded me.

A chair with a rickety back I'd been accused of breaking. You had to sit there without moving. My sister didn't mind and stared vaguely out the window. Today I realize that in all my memories of her, I see her in profile—the profile of a medal.

My aunt put a picture book on Guillaume's knees, always the same one, with the cover missing. We waited for my father. Before coming in, he banged his shoes on the doorstep, for a long time. And I never heard without inexplicable embarrassment the chilly, traditional:

"Good afternoon, Arthur. Sit down."

So, if they hadn't said that, he would have been condemned to remain standing. I was sure of it. It was an almost painful mystery to me.

The table was set, under the hanging lamp, before we arrived, with the apple tart in its place in the middle. By the window on the right was a sewing machine, always covered with scraps of fabric. And my uncle invariably smoked a cigar, which he kept relighting.

Actually, he was my great-uncle, my mother's uncle; she had been a Tesson.

And the Tessons of Saint-Jean-d'Angély always seemed to me a world apart, a world one must mention respectfully. When we passed a kind of château at the edge of the town, my mother never failed to sigh:

"That's where your grandfather was born! It would still be ours if it hadn't been for our troubles. . . ."

Is it possible that, for the past thirty-five years, I've never seriously asked my mother about these troubles? It's surprising only to someone who doesn't know her.

The little I know, I've guessed. My grandfather Tesson was a notary. He took risks. Not enough to go to jail, but enough to have to give up his practice.

And at the same time his brother, Aunt Elise's husband, gave up his practice as a lawyer.

He struck me forcibly. He was a small, thin man with a clubfoot, and he smelled of cigars but also of something else I couldn't define. But once during a quarrel I heard my father shout:

"He's an old lecher and stinks like a goat!"

My mother, distraught, looked at us, and didn't speak to him for a couple of days.

One detail comes back to me: the way my uncle Tesson's hands were continuously shaking. (Everyone called him "Tesson," even his wife; in fact, I don't even know his first name.)

I cannot say what the grownups talked about on those Sunday afternoons. But I can see them, each in place, my mother always looking slightly solemn, a vague polite smile on her lips to show her genteel upbringing.

What I cannot work out is what was so special about my aunt Elise. To me she was someone of my mother's age (thirty-one or thirty-two), and that was enough to put her in a definite category.

All the same, she was a rather remarkable woman. At least her presence in that solemn house was incongruous.

"How dreadful it is to see people like that come into the family," I heard my mother say one day, when she didn't know I was in the kitchen.

Aunt Elise was a tavernkeeper's daughter, and had been my uncle's mistress for a long time before she got him to marry her. She was plump, with a large bosom, and didn't dress at all like my mother. I would never have been able to say what my mother's figure was like, whereas one could always sense that the whole of Aunt Elise's body was alive; so much so that I actually blushed for no particular reason when she took me on her knees.

Was this why my mother told my father, in the carriage:

"I hope you'll manage to behave"?

I'd swear she did. I've never thought about it, but it was quite clear. And why do I remember something I'm sure I heard without being able to pin down where?

"Men think of nothing but their filthy business. . . ."

It was my mother speaking. To whom? I don't know. But she said it. She had a horror of the male.

If only I could relive one of those Sundays with the eyes and ears I have today!

My father, who hated sitting still, must have been uneasy in his chair. At home at Arcey, he was the biggest local farmer and had refused to run for mayor. He had only to speak and everyone agreed with him. Besides which, he was physically the strongest.

Here, that ugly clubfooted little fellow was the strongest, because he was a Tesson. No one dared contradict him, and he knew it. He must have done it on purpose, forcing my father to agree with absurdities.

Was it because strange currents were exchanged between my father and Aunt Elise across the room, which in spite of the tall windows was always dark?

"Shall we go to the table?"

It was Aunt Elise who spoke, getting up and helping my brother, Guillaume, to get down from his chair. With a single look, my mother reminded each one of us:

"Remember what I told you: only one slice of tart! And no more than two lumps of sugar in your coffee!"

It was so much a part of the ritual that we no longer took any notice. I never forgot the taste of the Saint-Jean-d'Angély coffee, which was quite different from the coffee we had at home.

Why was my father more flushed than usual that Sunday? My mother gave him a meaningful look. He was standing, tall enough to bump into the chandelier if the round table hadn't been underneath it.

My uncle Tesson, who never had come to the table with us, usually stayed in his armchair while we were eating.

"Aren't you going to sit down, Arthur?" asked Aunt Elise, surprised.

My mother coughed. My father didn't know where to put his big body, and his voice wasn't natural when he spoke.

"Well, Tesson, how about our taking this chance to go to your study for a minute?"

That has often come back to me since. And also the atmosphere at the farm during the previous weeks. Although, as a rule, our parents used to go to bed at the same time we did, right after supper, the lamp often stayed lighted during the evening. I heard the drawer of the dressing table in which papers were kept being opened and shut, and murmurings several times came through my sleep.

". . . go to your study for a minute . . ."

My aunt raised her head suddenly and frowned. I thought she was going to protest. My mother, on the other hand, behaved as if she had no wish to know what was going on around her. For a moment, life in the dining room was suspended, until Tesson murmured, making the springs of his armchair creak:

"All right . . . Come along now."

What aroused this sense of oppression, of painful unease, that took away all desire to eat? I looked around me and the room seemed to me huge and cold, with the pieces of furniture stuck in the corners, and the scene of the courtyard, beyond the windows, appeared dramatically arrested.

Did I really make a move to follow my father? Did I sense that there was danger somewhere? A look from my mother nailed me to my seat.

"If that's what you want," my aunt said, annoyed.

And her words also held a threat.

"Help yourself, Françoise."

The two men had had time to leave the room, to get away to that mysterious study.

"Why don't you take a whole piece?"

Hostilities had broken out. Aunt Elise glared angrily at my mother, who was cutting a slice of tart in two.

"Thank you. I'm not hungry. . . ."

My mother was looking at Guillaume, to whom my aunt

had given a large slice of tart. Guillaume knew what that meant and was on the verge of tears.

Things were going on below the surface that I didn't understand. My aunt suspected something.

"What's the matter?" she asked unpleasantly, her eyes moving from my mother to Guillaume.

"It's too big . . ." stammered my brother.

"It's nothing," replied my mother.

"It's your mother, isn't it? Who told you not to eat?"

My brother sniveled, not knowing which way to turn. He was scarlet, and I could see tears swimming into his eyes.

Listen, Elise . . ." my mother began.

"I've nothing to listen to. If you think I don't understand! I suppose the store tart isn't good enough for the Malempins. . . ."

"Elise . . ."

The atmosphere was so stifling that I wonder I didn't cry myself. The tart was there, huge and thick, a vulgar tart, in fact, bought at the local bakery. And it wasn't the first time this tart had given me nightmares. They used to discuss it on the way home.

"When a woman doesn't even bother with the housekeeping, she could at least make her own cakes. That horrible tart weighs on my stomach every time. One day, the children will get indigestion."

"You don't want any tart?" Aunt Elise said threateningly to Guillaume.

In her anger she spoke to him as though he were an adult. She made us all responsible for the silent insult she had just been given.

"What about you, Mémée?"

Oh, my sister's angelic voice answering:

"I like it very much, Aunt."

"What about you, Edouard?"

I made a sign that meant yes, then no—I don't know what.

"It's your mother who's been scaring you, isn't it? One day you'll be grateful for a store-bought tart. All I hope is that it won't be sooner than you think."

"Listen, Elise . . ."

"When you visit people to get money out of them, the least you can do is not spit on their plates. . . . If you don't like it, you can lump it."

Money . . . what money? Were we really there looking for money?

I'd never known such distress. I didn't understand. I imagined my father in the study, talking alone to Uncle Tesson.

Money . . . But why did we need money? Didn't we have the biggest farm and the nicest trap in Arcey?

My mother didn't move. I didn't dare look at her face, but as I stared at the tablecloth I saw her take her scented Sunday handkerchief out of her bag and wipe her eyes with it.

Aunt Elise was eating as if she wanted to eat for everyone, and poured herself some coffee so violently she spilled it in the saucer.

"It's a bit much, all the same," she grumbled, her mouth full, talking to herself.

Then she glared threateningly at the door, seeming to say:

"Just wait and see what's going on in there!"

One thing is certain: my mother didn't leave, she stayed where she was, in silence, and in the end picked up the slice of tart that lay on her plate and ate it daintily.

"There are folk who send their daughter to a convent and who . . ."

It was like the last waves of a storm, the tail end of increasingly muddled sentences, which Aunt Elise finally brought out without considering what they meant.

"Wipe your nose," my mother told Guillaume.

It was the signal for peace. Spoons went back into cups. We ate in silence, watching each other. My sister, with her fine white hands, held the food as delicately as if it were some precious object.

A door opened and shut at the end of the hallway. Then we heard my uncle's familiar footsteps, and a few short syllables. The dining-room door opened. The two men took their places without a word, and for a few moments the two women dared not look questioningly at them.

I don't know when or how we left. The lamps had been lighted, the curtains drawn. Cigar smoke made a blue cloud a little below the chandelier, and as my father rose, his head was above this cloud.

The maid must have cleared the table; I don't remember it. My cheeks were burning. My brother was again turning the pages of the picture book he knew by heart.

What can they have said? How did we say good-by, when it was dark outside? When we turned the corner of the street and the mare broke into a trot, my father probably wanted to speak, because my mother murmured:

"Not now . . ."

Because of us! Once we were home, everyone undressed, and my mother, in her petticoat, occasionally came into the kitchen to keep an eye on the soup. Eugène, the farm hand, loomed up from the cowshed when we sat down at the table, and, as usual, took his knife out of his pocket. It had a horn handle, and the blade was much worn because he amused himself almost every day honing it.

Something had been said, apparently, in a low voice in my parents' bedroom. They were both calmer, and tried to appear as if nothing was the matter. During the meal my sister was asked questions about the convent and about a friend from Saint-Jean-d'Angély who was at the same school.

My brother and I slept in the same room; he still had a crib. The room had been divided in two by a partition that didn't reach to the ceiling, and my sister, when she stayed at home on Saturdays and Sundays, slept on the other side of it.

Next day I would hear her getting up at half past five, in the dark, to take the train to La Rochelle.

There was a fireplace in the kitchen, but the cooking was done on an enameled stove. We didn't have a tablecloth, like the Tessons, but spread a piece of checked oilcloth on the table, and I can see two bottles of red wine on it, and thick stemless glasses.

My father, like the farm hand, used his own knife, which he took from his pocket and laid beside his plate. After the meal, he cleaned it with a piece of bread before closing it again.

A detail surprises me, too late. My mother milked the cows, morning and evening. And yet I have no memory of her roughly dressed, as countrywomen generally are. She never seemed like a peasant woman, and I wonder, now, if she wore clogs to go to the cowshed. If she did, they didn't take away her air of distinction.

This isn't just a rough, shapeless memory of childhood. What she was then she has remained. In Rue Championnet, I have never surprised her in sloppy clothes when she is doing her housework, and she would never go and buy a chop at the street corner without wearing gloves and a hat.

There was another thing about her that can't have changed, a thing I can't exactly define; something that means I would never consider asking her certain questions.

And it also explains my father's silence during meals. I have tried hard, but cannot remember a real conversation at the table. My father might talk to the farm hand, and my mother would appear not to hear.

Why, now that I am married and the father of a family, have I never missed a single day's visit to Rue Championnet, except during vacations? These visits give me no pleasure; and I am sure my mother feels no pleasure in them, either. Yet neither of us would avoid them.

My father was as uncomfortable at the family table as I am in the apartment in Montmartre.

And on that particular Sunday he was more than uncomfortable. He was unhappy, humiliated. His big body got in his way, as did his heavy shoulders and even his animal strength.

Perhaps he was ashamed of being a mere Malempin, whose chronically drunk father was gardener on an estate at Sainte-Hermine and wasn't allowed to turn up at our home unless he was sober. One morning I saw my mother make the old man let her smell his breath.

My wife is just back. She removed her coat, saying nothing, and took Bilot's temperature. In spite of myself, I felt annoyed again.

"Did the vaccination take?" I asked.

"Yes. Morin saw Jean and says there's no danger."

We were both a little on edge, for no definite reason. We never argue. I was in the wrong. I'd have done better to go out and get some air, or simply to open the curtains to breathe some from outside. The sun must be shining. Weren't we in June?

"Have you given him the serum injection?"

"Not yet . . ."

I knew better than she did when the time was to do it. He was my son. The whole morning he'd watched me writing, and he wasn't asleep. For a long time he would remain awake. And now that we were both near him, it was me he was looking at, me alone.

"Aren't you going to eat?" asked Jeanne, preparing to take over.

I hesitated. . . . No . . . Yes . . . Why was I thinking of the tart so intensely that I had the taste of it in my mouth?

"Rose has your lunch ready. . . . I'll eat later. . . ."

It was absurd: if I'd looked at her, she'd have felt a kind of defiance, seen the hostility in my expression.

And then there was Rose, clumsily serving me, so scared of the idea of infection that she was wondering whether to give notice.

"Why have you put out the good wine?" I asked her.

"It was madame," she said.

To sweeten me. Shouldn't I go and ask her forgiveness? But what for?

3

One detail leads to another, and so it is that, by means of Jaminet, whom I no longer think about, I've found a date, the only one so far. It's isn't the date of that Sunday at the Tessons', or the next day, or probably Tuesday. It isn't Thursday, either, because I wouldn't have been enjoying time off on a Thursday.

So it was Wednesday, that seems the most likely. "Time off" obviously meant not going to school, but there was something else as well, and it wasn't easy to get all the right conditions together.

I already had a large head, and at that time it probably looked out of proportion to my small body.

"Edouard, I never know what you're brooding about in that big head of yours!" my mother liked to say.

I should point out that although my brother was called "Guy" and my sister "Mémée," no one ever thought of giving me a nickname.

I wore black woollen stockings, clogs, a coverall of black

sateen, and a satchel on my back. A kilometer of rough, muddy road, between hedges (those hedges that scared me to death), lay between me and the school at Arcey; and I always walked that road alone, because no other child lived near our farm.

It's odd to see myself walking along it again, with my big head and serious, worried face, never hurrying, stopping to look at any odd thing and frowning with the effort of thought.

There was another thing they often said at home:

"Just ask Edouard!"

About everything and about nothing. For instance, five hundred yards from our house stood a hovel. The husband was a railroad worker. The wife, Tatin, was hardly ever at home. People used to come to our house and ask about her. And if I was there, it was I who answered:

"She's gone to see her daughter at Saint-Jean. . . ."

Or else:

"She's in the field cutting grass for the rabbits. . . ."

It seems I noticed everything, registered everything in my huge head. I now know that this is both true and untrue. The fact is that, in my own way, I entertained myself. I had made myself used to solitude. At school I had no friends, because I didn't walk there with the others.

I didn't observe—no! An object struck me, some small detail, a fly, a stain on the wall, and from there I started off on some long adventure that I told myself. I created personal joys for myself, small daily pleasures, even in class, for instance when I managed to get near the stove and gradually grew torpid and red-faced.

Time off was the height of bliss. I rarely managed to

achieve it, about once every winter, when I had flu, since it was a tradition to have flu every winter, and everyone had a turn, including my mother and my sister, who spent a whole week at home.

Another detail comes back to me, which I put down haphazardly. Apart from those time-off days, when I was at home, I stayed in the kitchen, like everyone else, because it was the only room that was heated. But I never sat on a chair.

"You're always on the floor, wearing out your pants!"

On the floor, yes, near the tall fireplace that, seen from below, became even more imposing; the fire in it seemed very important, too. That wasn't all. Other conditions were necessary for perfect happiness. I would manage to collect certain provisions, and possess, all at the same time, some chocolate, an apple, some gingerbread or a biscuit. Sometimes I'd add things that weren't for eating, but no less precious: a two-colored mechanical pencil I'd wanted for ages, a metal box full of buttons.

Sitting on the floor, my back against the whitewashed wall, I lined my hoard up around me so as to set up an imaginary frontier, and could spend hours there, biting occasionally into the apple and sucking away at its pulp, or letting a square of chocolate melt on my tongue, or a piece of gingerbread. What I saw most of my mother were her skirts. And inevitably my peace was spoiled by Guillaume, who tried to invade my territory.

I would defend myself. My mother would intervene.

"Will I have to put each of you in a separate room?"

The separate room, the splendid solitude—that meant time off, and this time, as always, it came about without any previous planning. The day was gray. It was raining. The cows had been mooing in the shed for a long time, and my morning sleep had the special taste of those time-off days.

"I think I've got the flu."

No one was surprised. It was that time of year.

"Stay in bed. I'll bring your medicine. . . ."

Not just the purge, an herb tea I didn't dislike, in spite of its bitterness, but all the other accessories of Malempin flu: an enameled chamber pot placed on an old piece of carpet, then a strange kerosene stove, or, rather, a big lamp, surmounted by a kind of drum made of metal that allowed it to heat the room, which had no fireplace.

"Now, Guy, don't go bothering your brother, and try not to catch his flu!"

A damp compress around my throat . . . On the bedside table, a jug with pink flowers on it, containing lemonade . . . I knew that at noon I would have the right to some baked custard, on a brown plate that was used only on flu days. And the door leading into the kitchen would stay ajar all day. . . .

What was odd was that every time I decided to take time off, I really did have flu, or anyway a slight temperature, a coated tongue, feverish eyes, strange dreams, and the feeling that everything was swollen, the red eiderdown, the pillow, my head, my stomach, and, above all, my hands, which became monstrous.

Kitchen sounds reached me, and noises from the cowshed, from the stable, from the coach house where, on that day, because it was raining, my father had set up the power saw to cut wood.

I could hear the toothed wheel attacking the bark, and imagined the sawdust, first brown, then white and creamy, the thin, straight cut, and finally the log falling. I could hear the clatter of crockery and the more nerve-racking noise of some small mechanism, the zoom of a train that Guy was pushing around the kitchen table.

I wasn't mistaken in saying it was a Wednesday. In fact, I'm quite certain of it because around nine o'clock my mother started ironing, and Wednesday was our ironing day.

From time to time, she poked her head around the half-open door. She didn't look at me, but at the chamber pot, saying:

"Still no result?"

My mahogany bed was very high, with two feather mattresses and an eiderdown that crushed me. I remember the cows that Eugène brought into the yard, a corner of which I could see through the window; and because of the rain Eugène had pulled his jacket over his head, which made him look extraordinary; the sleeves hanging down gave him four arms.

There are so many gaps in my memory, yet I can still see that image quite clearly, and I know, too, that I was on the pot, serious and patient, when the small horn yapped like a puppy in the lane. The iron fell off the ironing board, and my mother sighed with annoyance when she heard the shrill honking.

It was Jaminet, in his amazing car. The only thing I find surprising is that my mother didn't push Guy into the bedroom and shut the door at once; because when Jaminet had the notion of stopping at our house, she used to get rid of us in a hurry.

Why he was called "Jaminet" I never knew and never thought of asking. Since he was my father's brother, he should have been called "Malempin," like my father, because I never heard of my grandmother's being married twice.

Unless . . . It's perfectly likely! Was Jaminet, who was the elder, perhaps born before his mother's marriage?

It doesn't matter. He had a café at Sainte-Hermine, three miles from us.

"I forbid you to speak like Jaminet."

"You're as uncouth as Jaminet."

"You're no more intelligent than Jaminet."

All this was part of Malempin speech. And Jaminet certainly was an oddity—rough, hairy, with a long mustache, clothes that seemed to be draped loosely around him, and amazing eyes that laughed without laughing, and a voice like none I've ever heard since.

He was my mother's closest enemy. When he went into town, in his car, which had knocked over a number of people already, he would make a detour to visit us, though there was no reason for him to come, and he cared nothing for his brother.

I stayed on my pot, where I was happy to sit for ages. I heard the glass door of the kitchen open, and the extraordinary voice call gaily:

"Hello!"

Jaminet had a speech defect. He spat as he talked, making the *sh* whistle and dragging out the syllables. If I'd been there, he wouldn't have failed to pinch my ear and say, with his thick accent:

"And how's this young sharp one?"

Which, in his mouth, became "shaaaarp . . ."

Without further ado, my mother asked shortly:

"What's it you want now, Jaminet?"

Was it just a first name, as inexplicable as Bilot?

"To be frank, dear sister-in-law, I want to wish Valérie a happy nameday."

He was a voluble talker, especially when my mother was around. He would sniff with abandon, never using his handkerchief, and he enjoyed spitting on the floor, in a long jet, knowing that every time he did so she shuddered.

"Who's Valérie?"

My mother went on ironing, while Jaminet sat astride a chair.

"She's a kind of tart from the village of Huteau I go and see when I feel I've got an itch to . . ."

Three fast steps. My mother came and briskly shut the door between us, and I calmly moved the chamber pot close to the keyhole, to go on listening.

"Can't you watch your tongue in front of the children? I really think you do it on purpose."

No one bothered about my brother, who was thought too young to understand.

"D'you imagine they won't get wise to it sooner or later? My whore of a daughter . . ."

"Jaminet!"

"What? Haven't I the right to call my daughter a whore

when she's in trouble at the moment and can't even say who the fellow was?"

I knew that being "in trouble" meant being pregnant. But why, when I heard those words, did I think of Aunt Elise, who had never had a child? And why did I see her with my father?

"What else have you been up to?"

There, what I remember ends. I recall vaguely a sound of footsteps, no doubt those of my father, who had heard Jaminet's car and was coming to the rescue. He must have taken his brother into the coach house.

Later, I was curious enough to look at a calendar. The feast of Sainte Valérie fell on December 10. So it was on December 10 that I took time off, which puts the Sunday scene at the Tessons' on December 7.

It was only in the evening, when they lighted the lamp, the one with the green shade, that my mother realized I had impetigo.

My wife can't understand what's happening, and I sometimes catch her glancing at me anxiously when she thinks I don't notice.

Yet I'm very nice to her. I'm calm. I've always been calm, and I realize that I was equally calm when, at seven, I walked all alone to school, my satchel on my back, or when I took time off beside the oil stove.

At the end of the second day, Morin asked me casually:

"You don't want me to send a nurse?"

Jeanne must have spoken to him about it when she accompanied him to the hall.

"No. I'm no longer tired. The worst is over."

Still, I now seem more reasonable. I have my meals in the dining room and have just had a bath and opened the bathroom window. I've promised to go for a walk around the neighborhood tomorrow.

It's a pity, but all for the best. I've already set up my routine and the day seems well organized. I cannot find words to describe the mysterious intimacy that has established itself between Bilot and me; and this intimacy is all the stranger because he can't speak and I scarcely open my mouth.

He watches me coming and going. He sees me writing. Sometimes I give a start because I have a feeling he can guess everything I'm thinking, and then I stand beside his bed and smile at him, and turn away only when I feel my eyes become moist.

There's a subject I never touch upon, with Morin, or with Jeanne: the tenth day.

All three of us think of it: ". . . the serious symptoms as a rule appear about the tenth day, brutally, resulting in sudden death, accompanied by extreme pallor . . ."

Happily, care is now needed, rather than long hours. It gives a rhythm to our secluded life. The bedroom curtains stay drawn. The steam, which we keep going in the room, increases a sense of unreality.

It was I, just now, who gave Bilot a quick bath, to produce some reaction. And while I was holding him naked in my arms I noticed that he, too, had a huge head on a small, soft, milk-white body.

My wife, who's been to see Jean, tells me she saw Rose in the hall below talking mysteriously to the concierge.

"I'm sure she's not going to stay," she says.

She's not complaining; she never does. If Rose leaves us, Jeanne will take on all the housework without grumbling. She always accepts whatever happens calmly, and is resigned to it in advance. Perhaps she'd be surprised, even disconcerted, if catastrophes didn't turn up now and then.

Last year, when Bilot caught his little finger in the door of a closet and almost cut through the joint, it was she who, without losing her calm, bandaged the finger and took him off in a taxi to the doctor on Rue de Varenne.

Hadn't she, as a young girl, taken care, for years, of her brother, who had tuberculosis of the bone?

It never enters her mind that she's devoting herself to something or sacrificing herself. She does it naturally, because life, in her eyes, is nothing but a series of illnesses and troubles, in the midst of which she keeps her balance and a certain good humor.

I'd almost say that if I'd been as fierce—the word isn't right, but I can't find any other—as I was the first day of Bilot's illness, she'd have considered me to be another patient, and have done what she had to do, looking after two people instead of one.

When she saw me closing the notebook she asked:

"What are you doing?"

"Nothing. Taking notes . . ."

She didn't press it, yet it didn't seem natural to her. If I leave the notebook around, she'll glance at it, not out of curiosity, but to find out the reason for my mood and to improve things if necessary.

I know her reactions in advance. She'll shrug her shoulders. Is that all? Childish, nothing more! As far as she's concerned, I'm a big child who can only be relied upon to do a pneumothorax and remove stitches.

Which isn't very important, because once it's finished it's over and done with forever.

She has even understood (without guessing the reason for it) my need to be alone with Bilot. When she's been in the room for a while, and has tidied up, and her duties are over, she hesitates a little, looks around to assure herself that she hasn't forgotten anything, that nothing's left to do. She looks at me, too, perhaps expecting me to stop her from leaving, then says:

"I'm going to get on with the washing. . . ."

Or with the kitchen. Or with anything you like.

Rose came, shamefaced, to tell us—knowing we didn't believe it—that her mother was ill and she had to go back to her village. Jeanne at once got a checked tablecloth out of the cupboard.

The hardest thing, after such a long lapse of time, is to measure the time between one event and another.

I have dated quite definitely the Sunday of the tart and the Wednesday of my impetigo.

This is something quite unexpected, and a few days ago I'd never have thought it possible.

After those two dates, confusion sets in. It continued raining for days and days, that's for sure, because the fields were under water and later the flood level was marked on the wall at school.

It was gray and cold. The stove heated my bedroom, but drafts came through the cracks around the windows, and one market day my father brought back some padded material, which he put in himself.

I watched him all the time he was working. We were alone, as we seldom were. He didn't know I was looking at him. His face, very close to the glass of the windows, was harshly lighted.

Now, I'm going to appear ridiculous: what I discovered that time was that his nose wasn't exactly in the middle of his face. The way I've put it isn't quite right, of course. The nose, instead of being straight, was slightly askew, which gave an asymmetrical impression. This meant that to me my father had two different halves to his face. This face was fleshy, and very hard. On the other hand, I was amazed to see from my bed that his large eyes looked uneasy, the eyes of a man who wasn't sure of himself.

Was this because his eyes were a very light blue? Or because they protruded? Or because, as he nailed down the padding, he was afraid of breaking the glass?

I must have had a temperature, and it's quite likely that apart from my impetigo I really did have flu. I must have been ill for my mother to stop Guy from playing in the bedroom and to scold him if he became too obstreperous.

My health gave no cause for concern, though. And yet my father was anxious.

How long does it take to nail a piece of padding to a window? Not more than a quarter of an hour, I suppose. Which means that I took in all these impressions in this space of a quarter of an hour. Eugène had passed outside again, with his jacket on his head once more, and a smell of leek soup came in from the kitchen.

For the first time I felt I had been somehow deceived in looking at my father's face. It wasn't as firm or as masculine as I'd thought. He was vacillating. He was thinking of things that upset him. What could put out a grownup? What could make a man like my father vacillate?

While he was working, he happened to turn toward my bed a couple of times, and both times I shut my eyes, which meant a kind of betrayal, because I let him think I wasn't looking at him.

He sighed. Sometimes the furrow between his thick eyebrows deepened.

The window was narrow, with small panes like those you find in old houses. The wall was thick, the whitewash flaky. Outside, the weather was raw. And his big head filled the whole of the bright window, which looked like a picture frame.

My mother came in. She said something like:

"Not finished?"

Mechanically, because she always had to keep her hands busy, she rearranged my eiderdown and picked up a dirty cup.

It would be terrible to be wrong, the more so because my feelings when I had time off and a certain amount of fever were always a little on edge. But why, later on, have I often, just as I am about to doze off, seen my father again as I saw him that day, and every time felt uneasy?

I don't know if it's so for everyone: I have a—happily small—number of unpleasant impressions, scattered disagreeable memories, that come back to me now and then in half-conscious moments, when I go to sleep with an overloaded stomach, or wake up in the morning after having drunk too much the previous evening—a thing that rarely happens.

This is one of those memories: my father less firm, less of a man than usual, my father uneasy and, after my mother had been in, seemingly ashamed of himself.

The comparison isn't apt, but I must have looked the same myself when my mother surprised me doing something forbidden, as happened when I watched a little girl of three or four urinating in front of our house. For years this memory haunted me as the most shameful thing possible.

There was an *M* carved on the handle of the hammer. But, in contrast, I couldn't say how my father was dressed. Though I remember my mother's clothes down to the last detail, my father remains to me a block, an immovable statue. Except for that moment of anxiety.

That moment when he seemed to me to be afraid of my mother . . .

Or was he hiding something, which would change everything and be even more frightful?

It is absolutely impossible for me to place Uncle Tesson's visit in time, to within the nearest week or so. I have tried in vain to find some detail, like the feast of Sainte Valérie, which marked Jaminet's visit. I still had impetigo, but it isn't an illness whose length can be roughly estimated.

What I do know is that I was no longer in bed. However, I wasn't back entirely in the kitchen, and this seems to me odd, because my mother was economical and it's strange that she continued to keep the oil stove on in my bedroom, instead of having me in the general room.

I had used the eiderdown, spread in a soft red pile on the floor, to make a splendid throne. The reddish glow of the stove helped to surround me with a fantastic atmosphere. The door remained ajar, because my mother never lost her habit of keeping an eye on me.

The waters had risen. There must be some straightforward way of determining the dates. There must be a meteorological station in the district, where one might find the daily figures for that year, the exact levels. But I know I'll never find them.

It started with the pool below the stone basin used as a horse trough. Usually that pool was only three or four meters across and covered with duckweed, except in the place where the overflow of the horse trough dripped and a stretch of black appeared on the surface of the water.

One morning the pool was so big that it surrounded the horse trough completely, and the duckweed now formed only a small dark-green island in the center.

It was still raining. Eugène kept going back and forth with his jacket over his head, rolling large barrels. I didn't wonder what they were for, and discovered it only later. They were filled with water to keep them from floating, then stood up and spaced apart. They thus served as supports for a footbridge, which would allow us to reach the road.

It was exciting. None of it had anything to do with everyday life, and I wanted to stop being ill so that I could walk on the footbridge.

One morning, I heard talk about the milk. As a rule the milk collectors brought their truck to fetch the pails about a hundred yards from the house, because it was too wide for them to turn in our bad lane.

They hadn't come.

"They're stuck, near the hill," my father said when he'd walked back from the village.

Was this enough to explain the dread that weighed on the house?

I only hope I'm mistaken. I know that, sitting on the floor on my red eiderdown, with my legs tucked under my bottom and my face reddened by the glow of the huge oil stove, I was hardly taking part in the family's life.

But why did my mother give me chocolate when I asked for it? We never had a right to chocolate when we were ill.

Why was the kitchen door closed, thus isolating me from the others? And why did my brother several times spend the afternoon with me, when it was the rule to separate us, in order to avoid quarrels?

I was crammed with food and drink, with heat, well-being, and dreams. Never, since then, have I had the chance of wallowing so completely in confusion.

I was still made to drink lemonade, I still had purgative tea inflicted on me, and my tongue still remained furry. At midday, each day, I had baked custard, then, about four o'clock, biscuits dipped in sugared milk.

My mother gave me what I asked for as if, quite suddenly, it had become unimportant.

"They've closed the school."

I don't know who said this, whether it was the postman or someone else. The fact is that the school had to be closed because most of the children were isolated on the farms.

What did my father do all day? I can't figure this out. Apart from the time he put padding on the window, I don't remember seeing him more often than usual, although out-door work was impossible.

The fields were under water. If he'd sawed wood, he could have done so for only a few days; and Eugène would have seen to the stable and the cowshed.

He didn't take the trap out, either. I would have noticed if it had crossed the stretch of water that was beginning to surround us.

And yet he wasn't in the house. So, he must have gone somewhere. Not to the village, because, apart from Sunday after mass, he never set foot in the inn.

Another memory proves it: he was shaving more often. During the whole of that period, I don't remember having felt that his cheeks were scratchy in the evening, as they usually were during the week.

My conclusion is that he walked to Arcey and there took the train.

Going where? Doing what? And, most important, why was there a light in the kitchen until very late at night?

Why did my mother once say:

"You're no brighter than your brother!"

If she was referring to Jaminet (and my father had no other brother), that was dreadful.

And I was playing boats. The boat was my soft red eiderdown and the water was represented by the surrounding tiled floor. My brother had to pay to get a place on the voyage and for being set down on land. He had taken his clockwork toy to pieces and the wheels became coins.

The barrels were no longer any use, and the footbridge had been lifted onto blocks of wood.

When, how, and why did Tesson come to see us, particularly on his bicycle, which seems an unlikely thing for him to do? Yet I saw him crossing the footbridge wearing bicycle clips on his trousers. I'm sure the bike was propped up against the young elm in the lane. I'm also sure that before he came into the house my mother shut the bedroom door, without bothering to see what we were doing, my brother and I.

There was a long silence, like a period of waiting, and today I wonder: Where was my father?

4

Is it because dramatic moments are matched with confusion and surprise that they become bearable? I don't know, and if I try to set down the way the hours I've just lived through went, I can find nothing, either.

I was quite alone, and it must have been ten at night when I frowned, and raised my head, because Bilot's breathing struck me by its irregularity. I went to him, mistrustfully, knowing that as soon as I moved the dramatic process would begin.

Pulse forty-seven! With gaps, like those in his breathing. I didn't dare drop his small wrist.

I swallowed my saliva and wiped my face. I don't know why, but I put off the moment of waking Jeanne, who had only just gone to bed. My movements were calm and precise, as they are at the hospital when I am caring for one of my patients, but I was moving about in a spongy universe and kept saying stupidly to myself:

"I'm keeping perfectly calm!"

I'd ordered oxygen cylinders and went to get one from the living room. Once again I took his pulse: forty-four . . .

"Jeanne!"

She understood at once. I don't think she noticed my stupefied state, however, and took my calmness for confidence.

"Aren't you going to call Morin?"

"Yes . . ."

I telephoned. Deliberately I used ordinary, inane words.

"Forgive me, madame. . . . I'm very sorry to disturb you. . . . It's Malempin. . . . Yes . . . Your husband's not in? . . . At the Palais d'Orsay? . . . Thank you . . . I hope it's only a warning. . . ."

How many hundreds of people had telephoned me like this?

"Hello? The Palais d'Orsay? . . . You are having a banquet for physicians, aren't you? . . . Would you have Dr. Morin paged, please? . . . Yes. It's very urgent."

A little later Jeanne asked:

"Is he coming? . . . Is there nothing to be done while we're waiting?"

"Perhaps . . . Of course . . . But I don't dare. . . . Pulse forty-one . . . The vital signs are hardly noticeable. . . ."

My wife put on a dressing gown, fixed her hair, waved a powder puff, and went and opened the front door, waiting on the landing.

Morin turned up in evening dress; he had been at a big dinner in honor of a Brazilian medical delegation. He didn't ask me anything, treating me the way one treats sick people's relatives, taking no notice of me.

First he took the pulse. Then he removed his overcoat and pulled off his white tie before soaping himself up to the elbows.

The struggle lasted a little over two hours, with only a few syllables from Morin to ask for something. His waistcoat was off, letting the tabs and the bottom of his starched shirt stick out.

That was all. At ten to one, he looked at his watch.

"Too late," he murmured.

He was alluding to the Palais d'Orsay. He dressed again, not knowing what to say. My expression was questioning, and there's no denying it was the look of a patient.

"For tonight, anyway," he said.

It was enough. Bilot had a few hours ahead of him. Now I was able to say:

"Was there a good crowd?"

My wife filled some small glasses with liqueur, but Morin, who has a duodenal ulcer, refused. It was when he had gone that Jeanne looked at me with amazement. She was expecting anything except what I actually did.

"Where are you going?" she asked.

"I'm . . ."

Where was I going? To open the refrigerator. And I actually hesitated, as if out of greed, as I looked at the leftovers inside: some herring filets, a chicken leg, a piece of steak, boiled beef. I took the lot into the dining room. She saw me, through the half-open door, and couldn't understand.

I ate enormously, and drank a large bottle of beer, all by myself, gazing dully around me.

From time to time Jeanne shook her head, and I'm sure she felt impatient and sad. What could I have said to her?

Besides, it wasn't the first time she'd considered me like this. Our reactions are different. She's sure I'm cold and selfish, that I value my own well-being more than anything else.

What would she say if I told her what I was thinking just then? It came to me as I was crossing the kitchen and opening the door of the refrigerator. I had the feeling of seeing myself in the room and being surprised to find myself there.

How long had we been living in this apartment? A little over fourteen years. We furnished it room by room. In the dark, my hand quite naturally finds the doorknobs.

Why have I never had the feeling of being in my own home? That isn't exactly true. Thousands, tens of thousands, of doctors have an apartment that is more or less the same, get up at the same time, receive the medical journal I see on a round table, which is published by a firm that makes pharmaceutical products.

The waiting rooms look alike; so do the consulting rooms, give or take a few instruments. So do the vacations in the country and the once- or twice-weekly games of bridge . . .

All these are facts, of course. The proof is that I have conscientiously made the gestures I ought to make, at the right time. I behave like a good husband, scrupulously. I am a good father.

But this wasn't the first time I'd suddenly stopped, looked at myself, and wondered if the whole thing was real.

At one in the morning, after a fight like that, I was eating, and, what's more, eating with obvious greed!

Ah well! I could have said with almost scientific exactness what, as I crossed the kitchen just then, had given me that feeling of unreality: I hadn't noticed the *smell*.

Because, for me, the smell of any kitchen is that of our kitchen at Arcey, a smell of burning wood, fresh milk, and cowshed, a smell I've never smelled anywhere else and that in my subconscious is linked to the idea of family life.

Our kitchen in Paris doesn't smell. At least to me it doesn't. But I'm sure that to Bilot, to Jean, it has just as much smell as the kitchen at Arcey has in my memory.

While I was eating, I thought things over carefully, to recover. I was bewildered by the conclusions I was coming to. If I was right, the only years of real life are those of childhood.

And after that, just when you think you're seizing reality by the scruff, all you're doing is thrashing about more or less in space.

So, it's only Bilot who's really been living through these last days!

When I returned to the bedroom I was tactless or cynical enough to ask Jeanne:

"Aren't you hungry?"

She merely shook her head.

Did she know where I'd come from, she who didn't know the house at Arcey, who hadn't taken time off? And I'd never seen the little girl she was, either. We'd been living together for fifteen years and sleeping in the same bed. Yet what did I know of her inner life and what did she know of mine? It's true that she, who doesn't go looking for difficulties where there aren't any, sometimes looks at me as if she's seeing me for the first time, wondering, no doubt, what I'm doing beside her.

That's it! None of it matters. There's nothing to stop us from going on as we started, because that's how things ought to be.

"You'd better go back to bed," I said.

She hesitated.

"Are you sure you won't drop off?"

"I'm not at all sleepy. . . ."

She resigned herself, said good night, assured herself before leaving that there was enough boiling water. She left the door ajar; her trust was never complete.

Would things have been different if we had loved each other? We live like everyone else, like my father and mother, like Morin and his wife, like the various households of colleagues I know, except perhaps the Fachots. But then, Fachot married one of his patients when he couldn't hope to snatch her from death, thus infecting himself voluntarily, in fact.

I got married because I was twenty-eight and it isn't a good thing for a doctor to be a bachelor. It was in full awareness of this reason that I used to go to see my teacher Filloux on Thursdays. I knew that, if he asked his students to his apartment on Boulevard Beaumarchais, it was because he had four daughters to marry off.

He was gentle and dispirited, unsophisticated, his hair already turning gray. Jeanne seemed to have come straight out of a woman's novel.

"I've got to be honest with you. There is someone else."

We always brought this childish honesty, these bookish scruples, to our relationship. She told me about a young man, a neighbor, who had courted her for two years and finally told her:

"Deep down, I don't think I'm suited to marriage. I'm tempted by the colonies, adventure. . . ."

"And if I followed you?"

"I haven't the right to take on such responsibility."

He spent three years in Gabon, as agent for a shipping company, then married in Bordeaux. And I married Jeanne.

I'm not at all sure that I shall get at the truth. It's an aim, almost an excuse, that I gave myself at the start, but now I don't really mind. What gives me a perverse sensual pleasure, the way a toothache can do, is rediscovering each moment details I thought I'd forgotten. The cat, for instance. How could I have forgotten the black cat that always had scabs on its head and was chased out of the kitchen by my mother ten times a day?

"I forbid you to stroke that nasty creature. One day you'll catch some disease."

And when I got impetigo:

"I warned you. It's the cat. . . ."

For the date of the famous visit, I can find nothing. I can remember, though, complaints about my uncle from Aunt Elise.

"He's an odd fellow. He goes off for whole days on his bike, on business, and doesn't tell me where. . . ."

At the time, Uncle Tesson's affairs seemed to me mysterious and even awe-inspiring; and the mere door of his study was enough to impress me. Later, I never discovered anything further. What was the point? It was a case of a one-time lawyer turning into a rather shady businessman, as so often happens in small towns. Very likely he dealt in real estate, investments, management of other people's property.

He was suspicious of his wife.

I have proof that he was just as devilish as I took him to be when I was a child and ingenuous.

This ugly, lame creature, at around fifty, had married an amply endowed girl of twenty-eight, a fact that, to the family, that is my mother and her sister, who lived in Nantes, meant betrayal. In Malempin parlance, it meant theft. He stole from us an inheritance we were expecting, to which we had a right.

But the old lecher wasn't as rash as he might seem: on a tiny piece of tissue paper, he'd made a will disinheriting his wife.

I learned this detail later from my brother, Guillaume, to whom my mother had always talked more than she did to me.

I don't know why quarrels broke out between Tesson and his wife. Was he jealous? I don't think she was unfaithful, since she was a prudent woman and valued her position.

Unless . . . I'll go back to that later.

Whenever they quarreled, Tesson used to bring up the tiny will, folded under his thumbnail, which he grew very long. He would agitate this finger in front of Aunt Elise teasingly and repeat like a fool:

"Tiny, tiny, tiny! . . ."

Like peasant women calling in the chickens at night.

I didn't see it, but I believe it. The atmosphere in the house at Saint-Jean-d'Angély was suited to scenes of this kind. Guillaume maintains that my uncle's erotic tastes weren't quite normal and that, in bed as elsewhere, he used this kind of behavior to bring my aunt to heel.

Had he real vices? Very likely. In that case, he was the kind of man to use extraordinary precautions to satisfy them. This explains the old black bicycle, to which he remained faithful even when a car would have suited his business trips better. He must have been able to get about less obviously on the bike, and to have been more in command of his movements.

What worries me is one question, always the same one: Where was my father that morning? For it was in the morning, because I hadn't eaten my baked custard yet.

I also wonder if my mother was expecting his visit. My uncle seldom came to see us. Twice? Three times? Once, anyway, I was sent to the village to get a bottle of apéritif at the grocer's because the one kept in the sideboard for special occasions was empty and they didn't dare serve Tesson white wine.

But I'd swear he wasn't offered the traditional glass that day. I would have heard the sideboard being opened, the bottle uncorked.

On the contrary, after a fairly short conversation in low voices, my mother crossed my bedroom to go into hers. When she went through again, she was holding the worn gray wallet in which money was kept. She scarcely looked at us, but said:

"Be good, won't you?"

After that, a long silence, a gap. Were Tesson and my mother still in the kitchen? Were they looking at papers without saying anything? Had they left? And if they had left, where had they gone? Was it that I no longer heard anything, while they went on talking in low voices?

I know nothing about it. But I'm not giving up yet. I'm sure everything hasn't been completely extinguished in my memory, and that the sparks will be kindled again at the right moment.

I regain awareness only at the point when I heard Jaminet's honking in the lane. I looked through the window and could see no one, no bicycle. Then Jaminet shambled into the kitchen in his hobnailed boots, and in his drink-sodden voice called:

"Anybody here, anyone at home?"

This seemed to last a long time. I was even wondering what he was doing when suddenly he opened our door:

"Hey, you kids, is the whole place empty?"

At that same moment the glass door opened and my mother asked:

"What d'you want?"

"It's not you I'm after, it's your husband. . . . Isn't he here?"

Our door was shut again. By my mother, obviously. Less distinctly I heard some talk about two days with a man and a horse to go to collect material at the station.

It's quite easy to reconstruct the conversation. Jaminet never used a contractor. He tried to do everything himself, with the result that his café looked like a monstrosity. He'd got the idea of building a dance hall in the place of a disused chicken house. Since there was no work in the fields, he came and asked for the horse and cart, and my father's help, or Eugène's.

"Speak to him about it when he comes back."

He must have been in the kitchen when my mother crossed the bedroom again to put the wallet back in its place.

"You haven't been fighting with your brother, have you?"

No! I was absorbed. Sitting on my red eiderdown on the

floor, I had overturned a straw-seated chair. With the help of a nail found God knows where, I was inserting pieces of string among the straw, and I forget what this represented in my mind. As for Guillaume, he was somewhere around but I took no notice of him.

Two men's voices came from nearby, one of them my father's. So he was back, which cheered me. The house seemed more alive when I heard his voice.

"Tomorrow, that's no good. . . . But Monday . . ."

Does that mean it was Saturday? Not necessarily, Sunday being by definition an empty day. It might have been Friday. But it wasn't the Friday of the same week as Jaminet's visit on the feast of Sainte Valérie. If it had been, he'd already have mentioned the dance hall when he visited us on Wednesday. The idea didn't come to him in a couple of days.

Later we'll see how that fits in with the rest.

"Have a bite with us?"

He must have said no. I heard the car leaving. There was silence in the kitchen, although my mother and father were there.

Why didn't Jaminet mention Tesson, whom he knew and hated with a passion? Hadn't he met him, then? My mother, who was rather proud of her rich uncle, hadn't taken the opportunity of saying:

"Tesson's just left. . . ."

And she hadn't picked any quarrel with Jaminet, as she always did.

"Come to the table, Guy!"

Not me. I was ill. I had no right to the others' meals.

"You'd be better in bed. What are you doing with that chair? Are you crazy?"

But she'd walked across the room twice without worrying about what I was doing.

"I'll wash your scabs first. You can eat later."

A smell of disinfectant and the slight hissing of foam. Then the nastier smell of the salve . . . My mother turning me unceremoniously this way and that, gripping my face with her iron fingers . . . and her expressionless face, which I could see quite close to mine.

"You've let the wick smoke again. Your nostrils are all black. . . ."

She cleaned them out with cotton wool, which she twisted in her fingers; hurting me, pulling my skin. My neck stretched tight, I waited for her to finish.

Then, behind her, I saw my father, who had come noiselessly to the doorway and was looking at me. He said nothing. He was smoking his pipe, as he did after every meal. His large eyes were shining.

My mother, who must have felt his presence, turned:

"What are you doing here?"

I was deeply humiliated to see him meekly go back to the kitchen.

"If you scratch your scabs again, I'll tie your hands, d'you hear?"

Perhaps my mother doesn't remember them, but those words still sound in my ear, quite distinctly, like a phonograph record.

"Can't you sit anywhere but on the floor?"

It is because I remember her voice all too well that I feel, today, that she spoke without thinking, just to make a noise. She scolded without scolding. She took care of me somewhat in the same fashion as I stuffed myself after the fright Bilot gave us, a while ago.

The wind was blowing. I don't know if it was raining, but it was windy, because, when my father went out, the glass door of the kitchen slammed so hard behind him that I thought the panes would break, and my mother raised her head as well, and frowned.

What did I do until the police came? How much time went by? Several days. And the water hadn't gone down. I have proof of this: I amused myself fishing through the window with a piece of string and a bent pin on the end of a stick. My mother loomed up, shut the door behind her, took my fishing rod, and went back to the kitchen without scolding me.

At about the same time, Tesson failed to return home. Elise waited up for him all night (it was she who claimed this), then in the morning telephoned the hospital. Still, there's nothing to prove that the day Tesson vanished was the day of his visit to Arcey.

Why did Aunt Elise telephone the hospital and not the police?

"I thought of an accident right away," she explained. "Since he was so nearsighted, I was always scared seeing him go off on his bike. . . ."

She didn't think of us. Even if she'd wanted to call us, she couldn't have done so, since we didn't have a telephone. I wonder what she did all that day in her house on Rue du Chapître.

That evening, anyway, she took the train to La Rochelle to visit her sister.

There was simply nothing to be said for her sister. Aunt

Elise, despite her vulgarity, had a certain something. The fact that she was extremely attractive made people overlook a good deal.

Her sister, Eva, who lived with an old colonial sergeant major, was a caricature of the faded tart, all the less likable because she gave herself airs and was furious that no one invited her to visit.

She had a cracked voice, and with her excessive make-up —lips that looked bloodstained and eyes ringed with black— she made me think of a skull.

It's Guillaume, once again, who's told me about her. He stayed longer than I did in the home country. Among other things, he quoted a passage from a letter Eva wrote to her sister. Eva had bronchitis.

"I wonder if my sergeant major wouldn't be glad to see me croak. . . ."

Then, at the end of her letter:

"A big hug, and a cough to Tesson."

This because Tesson had never asked her to Saint-Jean-d'Angély, and once when he found her in the house, he left it without a word, waited outside for her departure, and afterward told his wife that if that creature set foot there again . . . followed, no doubt, by a rude gesture.

So, as far as I know, Aunt Elise spent the night in the sergeant major's small bungalow near the barracks. What did the three of them discuss?

Only the next day, that is, two days after my uncle's disappearance, did my aunt go to the police at Saint-Jean-d'Angély, accompanied by her sister in full warpaint.

I've heard those events recapitulated several times. One detail is rather surprising, although it may be understandable.

When she got out at the station, my aunt went straight to the police, without first going home to see if her husband was back.

She didn't mention us, in spite of that business with the apple tart. I think she was basically quite a nice woman.

What she said I've guessed from the measures they took: it was in the brothels of the nearby towns and in certain unsavory country inns that the police undertook their first searches.

Had my aunt good reason to think that Tesson went to such places? I rather believe—for no precise reason   that the idea had come to her at La Rochelle. Her sister or the lover must have said to her:

"Did you know that he sometimes came here for a good time?"

In any case, from that time on my aunt's life was, as it were, tainted by that horrible Eva, and this was something I minded greatly.

Was it because of a certain attraction I imagined existed between my father and Aunt Elise?

Partly, no doubt.

But also, I'm sure, because of the attraction that Aunt Elise—the essence of femininity—exerted over the potential man I then was.

She didn't realize it, nor, for a long time, did I. Her sister's presence disillusioned me more than twenty years of experience. Physical love, to me, remained linked with the image of Aunt Elise and her generous bosom, but the idea of punishment, of bondage, was represented by Eva and the lover I never saw.

Is he dead? Probably. As far as I know, he was a rough

fellow who'd earned his stripes the hard way during thirty years in Africa. Would Eva have managed to make him marry her if a better place hadn't turned up at her sister's?

How could I explain to my wife, who wakes up from time to time and lifts her head off the pillow, how could I make her understand that when I went to the apartment on Boulevard Beaumarchais knowing exactly why, when I listened to her touching tale of disappointed love, when I promised with comical solemnity never to refer to it again and to try to forget it, it was because of Aunt Elise and her sister?

It would be hard for me to admit, even to a man, that to me the words "make love" automatically evoke my aunt's flesh—fair, pink, warm, abundant, and a little slack, perhaps.

But there's also the caricatured version, Eva, whom I actually saw only fleetingly, but who all the same is engraved on my memory like a Félicien Rops. And not only because of her lover . . .

And now I wonder what Elises, what Evas, my wife knew? Or, rather, what male Elise, what male Eva?

Although we probably speak much the same language, and live together as closely as people can, sleeping in the same bed, caring for the same children, we are unable to communicate to each other the inner realities that match our behavior.

My father was a peasant, working as a farm laborer at the age of fourteen.

Her father was a well-known physician.

Her mother died of a stroke when she was very young, and she retains the image of someone tender and delicate.

My mother lives on Rue Championnet and uses every

imaginable trick to make me assist my brother, Guillaume, with money and the small amount of influence I have.

Even the thought of rain . . . It's raining this morning, shortly before daybreak, and I'm alone, conjuring up, in spite of June in Paris, the wooden blocks that held up the foot-bridge.

I take nothing tragically. The proof is that a while ago I went to the refrigerator and stuffed myself. It's a knack. Give an animal food and his balance is soon restored, a rather delicate balance you can keep a check on later.

That doesn't mean that you can't be carried away occasionally, and live through a day at a faster rhythm, like the one . . . Why, I can hardly say whether it was yesterday, the day before yesterday, or the day before that. You are caught up by a gust that gives you the feeling you're going to be flung into something new, and beautiful, and

But I knew perfectly well, deep inside me, that this wasn't true and that it wasn't enough to buy a new car and decide on a trip to the South.

The proof is that I wasn't surprised when Jeanne told me Bilot was ill.

What surprises her, and rightly, is finding me always calm, serene, and accommodating. It's seeing me eat a few minutes after nearly losing my son. It's seeing me when she wakes up, writing quietly in the notebook.

She cannot guess that these are little dodges I learned early on to trick fate with. She sees me with my large soft body, my big head and its rather blurred features, and falls into the same trap as my mother, who today still believes that Guillaume is the great man of the family.

5

I don't know what I was expecting to see, but I was surprised by the quiet of the kitchen, with the kettle singing. It was a long time since I'd enjoyed its warm peace—the well-polished stove (through a little opening I could watch the glow of red ashes) and the fireplace, its logs and its smell, the sideboard and its decorated pottery, and finally the chairs I knew better than anyone, down to the smallest stalk of straw, because it was by propping myself against them that I'd learned to walk.

The grownups must have looked with surprise at the door opening so slowly, and must then have had to look down to see the small, large-headed boy there, not daring to go forward or back.

My mother, who was standing, took my hand, without arguing, without a word, with the firm authority you see in mothers walking and, without turning, dragging a child along at the end of the arm, a child having a tantrum. Once again the door was shut. Warm air receded to its proper place. The holes were stopped up.

One of the policemen was sitting at a corner of the table, his legs a little apart, his cap on the back of his head. A glass was standing on the polished table in front of him, and my mother had made room by piling up her copper utensils at the other end of the table; it was her day for cleaning copper.

The other policeman also had his legs apart, but since there wasn't room for him at the table, he let his arms hang down, and a cigarette was smoking between his fingers.

"You say the last time you saw him . . ."

My mother, who was standing, had exactly the right degree of calm as she replied, looking at the big notebook in which the policeman was beginning to write with a purple pencil.

"It was last Wednesday. . . . What makes me sure of the date is that Jaminet, my brother-in-law, came along shortly afterward. . . ."

I saw that the policeman was writing conscientiously:

". . . *What makes me sure of* . . ."

My mother waited, peaceably. I wonder if I opened my mouth to protest or not. My first thought was that she was mistaken, but she felt me moving, turned toward me, looked at me.

"Yes, it was Wednesday," she repeated.

I don't say she gave me a silent order, that she stared at me in a special way. I didn't feel her distress, either. Her eyes didn't beg me. No! I repeat that she was calm, sure of herself, and that it was I who turned red.

". . . *came here a little later* . . ." muttered the policeman as he wrote.

I felt crushed. My mother seemed to me huge, monstrously strong, and serene. Didn't I think for a moment that she was mistaken, because of Jaminet's two visits?

Once she'd looked at me, I knew that she wasn't. The mistake was deliberate.

"He didn't tell you about any plans of his? He didn't tell you he meant to go off on some trip?"

How simply did she reply:

"No."

"I suppose there wasn't any argument between you?"

She smiled slightly, excusing the question.

"Never."

As for me, I felt something tremendous was happening around my small person. My thoughts had swollen just as my fingers, my whole body, the eiderdown, and the pillow swelled up when I had a fever.

Wednesday was the feast of Sainte Valérie, that is, Jaminet's day, the day of Jaminet's *first* visit. The second visit, the *right* one, had taken place several days later, on Friday at the earliest, and it was then that he turned up when Uncle Tesson had just left and there was nobody in the kitchen.

But if Tesson had come on Wednesday, he'd have gone straight home and his disappearance would have had nothing to do with us.

And suppose, just by chance, he hadn't gone out at all on Wednesday, and Aunt Elise had declared that he hadn't left the house on that day?

"I think that's all," sighed the policeman, whose glass had been refilled. "Wait . . ." He glanced at me. "I suppose you know nothing about this affair? . . . You know what I mean. . . ."

He emptied his glass, he buckled his belt, snapped the elastic around his notebook. The other policeman rose without a word.

"So long, Madame Malempin . . . Greetings to your husband."

My mother shut the door behind them, poked the stove, poured water from the kettle into a saucepan. She said nothing. She asked no questions.

I am going to write something very much exaggerated, yet less inexact than it might seem: from that moment on, my mother no longer looked at me. And, although I don't dare to say that it was because of what happened, for my part I always from that time considered her a stranger.

That day, in the presence of the policemen, in the kitchen where every cubic millimeter clung to my life, as it were, a secret was born between a woman of thirty-two and a still-feverish child.

My mother aged. I became a man. I have children. For years and years I've been to Rue Championnet every day. I shall go back there tomorrow or the next day. Every month, I pay my mother the pension she lives on.

Neither of us has ever said a single word about Tesson's visit.

She knows I know. We talk of this and that, like people paying a call. So much so that as soon as I arrive she feels obliged to take a glass from the sideboard and pour me a drink.

If I try to analyze the feeling I conceived for her that

day, I think I can find some admiration in it. But admiration without warmth, a purely intellectual feeling.

At that time, I didn't know everything. Even now, I know only bits and pieces of our family history, because we've always been shy and silent about important matters.

So, I was told:

"Your grandfather was very rich, but he had bad luck, and your mother was brave. . . ."

I accepted this courage as an article of faith, and because it fitted my mother's physical appearance, but I couldn't have said exactly in what way she'd been brave.

I have since found out. When my grandfather, who was a widower, died, my mother was five or six years old, and she was taken by the nuns into some kind of free school for poor girls, if I've understood correctly. When she was fifteen they found her a job as a salesgirl at a grocer's at Saint-Jean-d'Angély, a big shop with two windows, always rather dark and smelling of the coffee they roasted themselves, which we passed dozens of times without her ever remarking on it.

It would seem that she was treated more like a domestic than a salesgirl, and that she slept in the attic.

It was there that my father met her, which explains why a Tesson agreed to marry an ordinary farm laborer.

Once, only once—I forget what about—my father lifted a corner of the veil and told me:

"You must never forget that your mother has been hungry."

The person who hasn't forgotten is she. Nor her humiliations.

Would my father, without her, have been ambitious, overweening, as they thought him in Arcey? He had a terrific appetite for life and its pleasures. And he had certainly decided not to remain a farm laborer all his life.

But his rise would have been different. I could feel, at home, what the Malempin element was and what the Tesson. I still feel, with a shrinking feeling, the difference that existed between our farm and the other local ones.

This difference was my mother, the dignity she gave, as if unwittingly, to everything she touched.

We ate in the kitchen with the farm hand, yet, in spite of the pocket knives the men laid on the table, these meals were a real ceremony, just as they were in Uncle Tesson's respectable dining room.

Apart from Jaminet, who did it on purpose, just because he wasn't sure of himself, I never saw anyone behave crudely under our roof.

This detail may seem silly. At other farms, when someone turned up unexpectedly, they took a bottle out of a cupboard, either wine or liquor, depending on the time of day.

At our house, there were rituals to which we conformed on every occasion: the postman, the neighboring farmers, country people, all had a right to white wine. However, if it was Sunday, and the visitor did not drop in but had been invited, there was vintage Bordeaux. The policemen who came now and then about chicken stealing or some formality were given liquor from a carafe, a cut-glass carafe that had a silver tray and six tall glasses. The same carafe was used for all the men on New Year's Day. And finally, someone from the town, like my uncle Tesson, had a right to a sweet liqueur and, because of that, to dry biscuits.

I never knew, although I was born there, the first farm

my parents rented, not at Arcey, but at Sainte-Hermine, near Uncle Jaminet's. We often passed as near as five hundred yards to it, but we never went out of our way there. I was told that it was a hut in the middle of fields and that there was only one habitable room in it; my mother must have given birth in the kitchen, and a door opened from there to the cowshed.

While we lived there my mother went into town at five every morning, summer and winter, to deliver milk from door to door. On the day before her confinements, she still did her round.

I'm certain, because I know her, that she was then just as stately as she is in her apartment on Rue Championnet.

Did the idea of buying the farm at Arcey come from her? Or from my father?

It was my brother, Guillaume, only a few years ago, mind, who said, when we were talking about something or other:

"It was that house that was their downfall. It was too expensive. They had borrowed money all over the place, and paying on time must have worried the life out of them. . . ."

In one of those regular panics, did my parents decide to get rid of Tesson?

I'm asking this question and trying to answer it with sincere detachment, though that isn't my usual attitude.

The crime in itself, if there was a crime, doesn't affect me, and I consider it without horror.

What has caused me to stir up these memories is a complex feeling, which becomes a little clearer to me only as I move ahead. It began with Bilot, with that weighty look he fastened on me, and with the Dr. Malempin I discovered in the mirror.

In any case, it doesn't matter. I am now wholly involved in the roots I'm untwisting, which I find keep going down farther and becoming more and more tangled.

It isn't a matter of knowing whether my father and mother had a motive for ridding themselves of the clubfooted Tesson. It was obvious. In the village everyone was aware of it. What surprises me is that the magistrates didn't start their investigation sooner, because, as far as I can remember, weeks went by before my parents were summoned to Saint-Jean-d'Angély.

What surprises me more is that Aunt Elise, who had no love for my mother, didn't put the investigators on her track.

Had she already forgotten the apple tart and the two men's memorable meeting in my uncle's study?

Tesson had lent us money. Not out of family feeling, of course. He must have lent it to plenty of people, at high rates of interest. Isn't that what the peasants call a "businessman"?

Did my parents need more money to pay interest elsewhere? Were they asking only for the renewal of bills that had come up for payment?

That might explain my father's shamefaced air. He was proud of his strength, of his ability to work, of his qualities as a farmer, which no one questioned. And now his big hands had to deal with alarming documents, his huge carcass had to bow to that ugly little Tesson!

It does no harm to his memory to say that his spirit wasn't subtle enough for these ploys. How could he be made to understand that what his gigantic labors produced went entirely to people who did nothing, and that the more he sweated the more he got into debt?

Was it that, deep down, he didn't care for my mother?

I've often thought about it. For years, I've tried to reshape the figure of my father, the man who matters most to me, yet whom I know least. Sometimes I shut my eyes. I try to see his face again and cannot do so. I make out an outline, no doubt bigger and broader than it really was. I say to myself:

"That's what he was like, with his nose like that. . . ."

And the image fades almost as soon as it appears. God knows why, but we haven't a single good picture of him, only one of those dismal enlargements touched up in soft pencil made by itinerant photographers in the country for the price of a gilt frame.

When he met my mother, he must have been proud of taking out a girl from the town, a girl who was educated and refined, with genteel manners.

If I'm right about him, he felt sorry for her, too. He was happy to protect, to feel needed. At the start of their marriage he probably didn't realize that he was nothing but a farm hand in his own home. He left it afterward, when it was too late. He must have worked it all out, realized in detail what he'd come to.

My uncle Jaminet's sneers were symptomatic. He guessed the situation and he knew his brother.

"Big mouth!" he said one day.

And, as happened with everything else, I took years to understand, but I didn't forget the words.

Jaminet meant that my father was a show-off, like any

man in a village who feels stronger than the rest. I never saw him at the inn, but I can imagine him walking in, with the assurance of a man aware of his own importance, shouting more loudly than anyone (he had an outsize voice) and giving his views on everything.

He loved amorous adventures, girls to be had in the back rooms of inns, but he had to hide it.

In spite of everything, wasn't it the very woman he was afraid of who gave him most cause for vanity? Of course he'd gladly have put up with more untidyness, a more easygoing home and way of life. Some constraints weighed heavily upon him.

But it was thanks to these constraints that our farm wasn't an ordinary farm and that at Arcey we weren't considered at all like peasants. We were clearly on our way to the country middle class, and in some people's eyes our house had the attractions of gentility.

All this was due to my mother. It was she who wanted us to be educated. It was she who sent my sister to boarding school at La Rochelle. It was she who planned that I should go to the lycée and to the university.

An insignificant detail: our clothes. As far as my father was concerned, our clothes were always good enough. It was my mother who struggled to give us a taste for fine dressing. It was she who, at the least sign of an ailment, sent for the doctor, though my father didn't bother.

He was innately selfish. He scarcely knew us, my brother and me, and in the evening, instead of paying attention to us, he thought up tricks he'd use next day on one of his sallies to a nearby village.

Why, then, is it with my mother that, even now, I mentally settle accounts? Anything connected with her, anything she did, I instinctively examine with care. I still can't keep myself from looking coldly at her, like a judge.

I can't possibly have been ill for so long. Yet I wasn't back at school. The water had gone down, leaving mud and dirt everywhere, nameless rubbish and the bodies of animals.

Were the Christmas holidays not yet over? I don't remember Christmas and New Year's at all that year.

One day the postman brought a greenish paper that wasn't in an envelope, but was folded and fastened with a stamp, like tax assessments, which produce gloomy discussions. My parents discussed it. I was half asleep when my mother came into my bedroom and prepared my good suit, which, with the right underwear, shirt, and shoes, was put on a chair to be ready for when we set out early next morning.

We dressed by lamplight. My brother wore his everyday clothes, but was lifted up into the trap with us.

That perfectly rational detail struck me, possibly scared me. I don't know what I imagined, but I wasn't far from thinking that my parents might have criminal intentions toward us. The world was damp and cold. It wasn't yet daylight. My neck and the lower half of my face were wrapped in a thick scarf, and my mother said as she put me on the seat:

"Be good, now!"

We stopped at Arcey and left my brother with an old woman, Mère Renaud, who had come to work for us during my mother's confinements.

Why did they take me with them to Saint-Jean-d'An-gély? I still can't explain it. Or, rather, I think that, from then on, my mother was always afraid I might talk.

The sun was rising as we reached the town. At one point, my father turned around to check something in the trap, and I noticed he smelled of alcohol.

We had stopped at the station. Once again, I was scared. I had a feeling they wanted to get rid of me.

"Come in. . . ."

Not the station, but an empty café that had its lights on. We sat down at a sticky table. My mother opened a package containing slices of bread, and we were served coffee, into which my father poured rum.

"Now, you'll be good at your aunt's. . . ."

So they were taking me to my aunt's? My father looked repeatedly at his big silver watch. A little later, we got out of the trap on Rue du Chapître and he unhitched the mare, Aunt Elise appeared on the steps, my mother jumped down, and they fell into each other's arms, sniffling.

"My poor Elise!"

I noticed a presence behind the curtain: Aunt Elise's sister, who didn't show herself any more just then.

"Would you mind keeping the boy for a while?"

Aunt Elise took my hand. My parents set off on foot.

They were going to the law court, to which they had at last been summoned.

As far as I can figure out, about three weeks had passed since my uncle disappeared. Why this judicial slowness? One mustn't forget that he had merely vanished. They might have thought he'd gone on a spree, considering the rumors about his behavior.

As for Aunt Elise, I learned later that she didn't tell the police.

Was it apathy on her part? Did she, too, for a while, entertain the idea that he had simply made off? Was she afraid of getting involved? Did her sister, who was suspicious of the police, advise her to keep silent?

One mustn't forget the business of my uncle's will, either; the will under his nail that he waved fiercely and that others, besides ourselves, might have known about. But no one mentioned this will any longer and Aunt Elise remained his sole heiress.

The morning I spent in the house on Rue du Chapître was one of the most memorable of my childhood.

I didn't know why I was there. My fears of the morning hadn't entirely gone. When I went into the dining room and saw the woman I had already glimpsed behind the curtain, I was really frightened.

I had never seen a creature like her before. She was wearing a bright-blue dressing gown, which she let hang loosely over her thin body. Her feet were bare in slippers, which she scuffed across the floor. And she smoked one cigarette after another.

"Aren't you hungry?" Aunt Elise asked me. "What would you like to eat?"

And there and then, for no reason, she kissed me and pressed me to her warm bosom, making me feel steeped in a mysterious feminine moisture.

"I've eaten, Aunt."

"Where did you eat?"

I blushed, remembering the tart. I didn't want to admit that we had stopped in a café to eat slices of bread.

"I don't know. . . ."

"There, you haven't eaten! Sit down here. . . . Do you like honey?"

She had the weepy sentimentality that women think ought to be shown after disasters. She had no idea what to give me to eat. For no reason, she kept kissing me and saying:

"When I think of your poor uncle . . ."

Even today I am astounded at the thought that it was there, in that house, with that woman, that my parents left me while they went to the law court.

I have imagined plenty of reasons for it. Contrary to what one might think, I have rarely, indeed almost never, thought coldly about these events. But sometimes images have turned up in my mind, some of them quite unexpected ones.

Such as, for instance, my father and Aunt Elise in each other's arms, in that very room, an image I saw in dreams on several occasions, with long intervals between them.

It's possible! I'd even say that, in a confused sort of way, I wished for it. But from there to believing that Elise would have asked my father to get rid of Tesson . . .

I think the explanation is simpler and better suited to the spirit of the family, the atmosphere we lived in. I'm sure that Jeanne, who lived an even closer family life, would understand it.

Isn't it for the same reason, among others, that she spends several hours a week on what she calls her "mail"?

In her big sloping handwriting, she writes pages and pages to relatives she has lost sight of, to childhood friends;

I don't know what she finds to tell them, but for her it's a sacred duty.

It is more a matter of discipline than of deception. The family is the family and one must behave in this or that way in these or those circumstances. For instance, at home, we didn't kiss each other once or twice, but three times, once on the left cheek, once on the right, then once again on the left.

A disaster had befallen us: so, one had to behave as one did in cases of disaster. And, in cases of disaster, the family is forced to forget its quarrels and hatreds.

I saw another instance of it. My mother's only sister, whom no one mentioned to me for years, and who even afterward was referred to in an ambiguous way, had married a waiter. They lived in Nantes and, if my mother wrote to Aunt Henriette, she never referred to him.

But when the waiter had an operation (for what illness I don't know), my mother set off for Nantes without delay. Though, later on, when my uncle was better, there was no mention of him in letters or in the family.

For weeks we saw more of Aunt Elise than ever before. The weeks, I suppose, during which the investigation lasted. And Aunt Elise received us with warm, melting, bathlike affection. On the sideboard there was a bar of chocolate exclusively for me.

Were my parents scared?

Did Aunt Elise fear suspicions?

That morning, spent in close contact with two strange women, was like no other. It was marked, besides, by an important event. I don't know when it was that my aunt and her sister went upstairs, after putting on my knees the picture book generally given to my brother. Above my head I heard footsteps and voices. It was dark, as always in that house, and I was bored.

For the first time, I went upstairs. On the landing I was surprised by a ray of sunshine. A door opened into an equally sunny room, blindingly bright because its walls were painted white. It was the bathroom. I saw Eva's blue dressing gown. She was busy dealing with a gas hot-water heater that she couldn't make work or adjust, and my aunt, completely naked, stood beside her.

She turned and saw me. She murmured:

"What are you doing here?"

And she came and shut the door.

We had lunch on Rue du Chapître. Aunt Eva (because that's what Aunt Elise had told me to call her) had changed into a suit that made her seem even more strange-looking, as if she were traveling.

They were talking about the magistrate, and my mother said:

"He was very polite. . . ."

Did he question my parents about their financial affairs? Most likely. If he did, my mother must have answered, while my father watched her admiringly.

Were they really suspected of murder? Again, most likely. I wonder what the magistrate can have thought of my mother.

She must have impressed him with her coolness. Did he realize that beside her my father didn't exist?

I know nothing of all this, but I suspect Guillaume learned about it later, perhaps from my mother herself.

We ate squab with peas. At the table, they spoke of my sister. My mother said:

"I'd prefer she stay at La Rochelle *until this is all over!*"

Why did she look at me from time to time, as if to guess from my face what might have happened during the morning? Why, on the other hand, did my father and Aunt Elise avoid looking at each other?

"I must give the boy something to remember his uncle by. . . ."

And after the meal we went into the huge empty study. Aunt Elise searched around her.

"I must give the boy something to remember his uncle by. . . ."

I was thinking of the watch, a gold watch that Tesson pulled out of his pocket from time to time (it was almost a ceremony), slowly opening its double case. Then he pressed a spring and the watch struck the hour.

It didn't occur to me, that afternoon, that the watch had vanished with my uncle.

"What can I give him that would be nice? . . . Let's see . . ."

"Don't go looking, Elise," my mother protested politely. "You can do it another time. . . ."

My aunt went on stubbornly looking around her in a kind of distress, and at last swooped on a fountain pen.

"His pen! There, that'll remind him of him. . . ."

"It's much too much. . . . Wake up, Edouard. . . . Thank Aunt Elise. . . ."

I was ashamed to kiss her, now that I'd seen her naked. Moreover, I was embarrassed at being hugged to her bosom.

My parents never thought of the pen again. When I got home I tried to fill it. It was encrusted with purple ink that had dried. I cleaned it with the care I always use in manual work, but when I tried to fill it I couldn't.

Yes . . . No! . . . When Bilot has recovered (I touch wood), I'll buy him a gold watch that strikes the hours. Once again his mother will look at me without understanding.

6

She asked me with feigned indifference:

"Going out?"

No, old girl, or, rather, my darling. It's just that this morning I felt a smell of indoorness, of fever and sweat, coming from my skin. I had a bath and the sun followed me into the bathtub. I shaved closely, put on my dark-blue suit, a clean collar, a tie, shoes, and socks.

When I came to put on the shoes, I hesitated, but really felt the need to have something on my feet that wasn't weak and soft, like slippers.

There! That was all! Morin was wrong, like everyone else.

"Going out?"

To hear her, you'd think I was the invalid. No, I wasn't going out. For the time being, Bilot was fast asleep. You couldn't say he was saved, because the most serious complications usually occur around the tenth day. But at least the serum had worked.

In this emergency, I was almost being looked at askance. Sunshine was pouring down from the sky, streaming in everywhere. The living-room balcony window was wide open. On the sidewalk opposite, I saw a wine merchant in an apron watering his end of the terrace to settle the dust. The street noises came in unmuffled, and, after spending several days in a closed room with the curtains drawn, I had the feeling you have when your ears have just been cleaned out.

In contrast with my clothes, Jeanne was wearing a gray apron which she'd bought recently to do the housework in; she had tied her hair in a piece of gray cloth, and just now, in the kitchen, I caught a glimpse of her wearing rubber gloves. She came and went, opened and shut doors, let in drafts, brought and removed brushes and dustpans and buckets.

Someone rang the bell. Since we now had no maid, it was she who went to open the door. In the bluish half-light of the hall I saw the man who each week comes to collect the laundry. He and Jeanne were bending over a big heap, counting the number of items.

There was another ring, the telephone. I picked up the receiver.

"Hello."

"Hello. Is that Dr. Malempin's? Could I speak to Madame Malempin, please?"

It was my mother. I recognized her voice, although it was distorted in the transmission.

"This is Edouard," I said.

It was rather as if I'd disturbed the established order.

In the hall, Jeanne raised her head. On the other end of the line, my mother didn't know what to say.

"Jeanne isn't there?"

"She's busy."

Nothing extraordinary was happening, I knew. Nothing at all was happening. Jeanne, who was finding the house-work took up a great deal of time, had decided not to go to Rue Championnet every day to see Jean. So it was arranged that my mother would call every morning at about eleven.

And, as Jeanne likes fixed arrangements, my mother was to take Jean in a taxi to the Champs-Elysées, telephone us at home, and then take him to the Bois for an hour or two.

Why to the Bois? Because the air in Montmartre was contaminated. Too many neglected children running about the streets and heaven knows what diseases he might pick up!

"Is Bilot better?"

"Yes."

"Good. So is Jean. . . . Tell Jeanne I'll call again soon. . . ."

What is hard to believe is that this was the first time I'd heard my mother on the telephone. So she must have had the same impression that I had, that of recognizing me without entirely recognizing me, feeling I was so far away that she could only stammer:

"Well . . . that's it, then . . . good-by . . ."

Jeanne had finished with the laundryman and was beside me.

"Didn't she say anything?"

Then something happened, something that really belonged to our home: because, in my patch of sunlight, I had a vague smile on my lips, Jeanne thought she was obliged to smile, too, out of politeness, as you smile politely at someone you don't know who greets you in the street.

Then she went on from there, asking me what I wanted for lunch.

Has she wondered why I married her? And, if she has asked herself the question, what was her reply to it?

Here we are, very nice to each other, each of us looking after the other, in this apartment that belongs to us and today had an aerial look about it, with its windows open and gusts blowing in all directions.

Since this morning I've been thinking very carefully that I chose my wife as if from a catalogue. She can't guess that, and she mustn't.

But it's true. She has *always* reminded me of those advertisements set out with a great many abbreviations: "Rfd yg ly, gd educ, musl, qt, hmlvg, sks gtlman . . ." ("Refined young lady, good education, musical, quiet, home-loving, seeks gentleman . . .")

And that was what I wanted. I wasn't talking nonsense when I mentioned a catalogue. When I thought of marrying, I thought of those catalogues with gay, sweet young women on the covers, wearing sweater sets or else dresses they made themselves from paper patterns.

I thought of those poignant advice columns: "Babette's Page," "Advice from Aunt Monique."

It was thus with fully conscious intent, you might say cynically, that I used to go to Boulevard Beaumarchais, where the parties given by my teacher Filloux were like those described in novels for young girls.

". . . would like to marry refined gentleman, civil servant or professional, liking children . . ."

And that's what I became. For fifteen years, I've been so carefully the man Jeanne might have dreamed up that she's sometimes watched me secretly, with some uneasiness.

However, that's what I was even before I met her. If I chose medicine rather than any other profession, wasn't it because it represented the security, both intellectual and material, that I wanted above all?

It is the same collector's tenacity that I carry into the smallest acts of our life, our vacations in Brittany, the small dinner parties we sometimes give, the bridge evenings, my clothes; and our furniture, the decor of our life, might also have been chosen from a catalogue, including the ornaments.

When we had Jean, I bought a camera, and we have photographs of the children at all stages, some of them enlarged and framed.

I'm gentle. All my patients agree that I'm gentle. I don't go so far as to say that this gentleness is artificial. I hate pain, and, even more, the sight of pain. I do anything to avoid it for my patients and also to allow them to avoid the most searing pain—that is, fear.

At the hospital they're fond of saying:

"With Dr. Malempin, you don't feel a thing. . . ."

And no one, not my wife, not my colleagues, suspects that this is a kind of pose. I mustn't exaggerate, though. Words are so precise that they always go too far.

A comparison would be truer. A patient used to his illness, especially a sick person subject to acute crises and knowing that they may seize him at any moment, lives prudently, walks gingerly, always ready to withdraw into himself. He feels that the pain is there somewhere; he doesn't know how it will pounce on him, and so he's cunning, on his guard, feeling his way along, as if thus hoping to cheat fate.

Like me, such a man must sometimes have a feeling that the universe isn't very solid, and must wonder if things are really as reliable as they look, if the real is really real, if voices are voices and if they belong to the people who open their mouths.

"Lunch is served," Jeanne announced, having taken off her working clothes and, in imitation of me, changed into something elegant.

I ate. I ate a lot. I ate so much that once again she glanced at me, and, to cover her glance, quickly gave me a smile.

The meal wasn't over before I was thinking of my notebook, and I was delighted to draw the curtains.

What I must say, what I want to say, forcefully, because in my heart and soul I'm convinced it's true, is that the events I've set down weren't the cause of what happened later.

Besides, what did happen? As you tell of your life, you easily come to believe, and to make others believe, in an exceptional destiny. Whereas I'm sure that thousands, tens of thousands, of people play games with fate as I did, deceive themselves, adopt attitudes because they think them the most suitable or the least dangerous.

What have I really done, anyway, except dimly follow a family instinct, the same that made my grandfather a notary in Saint-Jean-d'Angély, that urged my poverty-stricken mother toward a bourgeois life, or at least toward something that looked like it, had some fake similarity to it?

What I am, I was before the events at Arcey. The proof is that school, for instance, always seemed to me just as unreal as my apartment does today. I can hardly remember the other children. And I wonder how I can have spent so many hours, hundreds of them, in that country classroom and have remained impervious to outside things.

Why did I never say anything, never ask my mother or my father any questions? Why, later on, seeing it was so easy, did I never try to find out?

Admittedly, I knew. In the end I went back to school, in my clogs, the woollen stockings knitted by my mother, and my thick hooded cloak, and with my satchel on my back.

That morning, I followed the rough lane leading to the village slowly, stopping occasionally, the way I used to. I know that state of mind, because even now, while I'm walking, while I'm in a car, while I'm doing anything at all, I sometimes remain in abeyance, as it were, and when this happens I can't say exactly what thoughts have broken in upon the mechanisms of life.

Five hundred yards from our house, near a curtain of poplar trees, there was an unfenced piece of ground to the right of the road, where local people came to dispose of their garbage and trash, a shapeless evil-smelling pile of rubble and moldy vegetables, old buckets, iron bedsteads, tin cans, and dead cats.

I was entirely alone. You couldn't see the farm or the bell tower of Arcey from there, and it always made me feel slightly uneasy.

Yet I stopped. I don't remember stopping, or having

walked from the house to the rubbish heap, but I do remember a kind of brutal awakening.

I was looking at an object, perhaps for a long moment, and that object became a round, dirty cuff. I made out a gold button, with the small red dot of a ruby, and I recognized it. That button, that cuff, had belonged to my uncle Tesson.

I stayed there a little longer, I'm sure of it. I was trembling. I was afraid. Staring at that piece of white linen dirtied to darkness, I remained rooted to the spot. Then I started running as fast as I could. As I reached the village, I crashed into someone.

"Where are you going?" a rough voice said to me.

I was late. In class, they were repeating a lesson aloud, and I went into the humming sound as into a cathedral, hearing the teacher say:

"Malempin, you've got a bad mark. Go and sit down. Open your history book at page twenty. . . ."

The period that follows is more confused. Logically, there should be images of spring coming back to me, because we were in March or perhaps April. But there's nothing. Of our house at that time, I can remember hardly anything. It seems to me, though, that my father was often away and my mother sometimes went and met him by the roadside and they chatted softly before getting back to the kitchen.

I heard talk of a doctor. He didn't come to the house, but my father went to consult him, and from then on, at each meal, he took drops in half a glass of water.

"Don't forget your drops!" my mother kept saying.

Eugène, the farm hand, left for his military service, and we took on another servant, whose name I don't remember and who had epileptic fits.

For me, those weeks were concentrated on the rubbish heap. I no longer dared pass near it, and made a detour across fields, preferably along places where the farmers were working. So now I see once again large horses outlined against the sky, and men and women watching me going through the crops.

"Where have you been walking? You've got mud up to your knees!"

I didn't answer; I was silent. My mother never pressed me.

I didn't yet know that I was going to leave home forever, and when I remember my departure I become confused again.

What would I have become if I had stayed at home? But how much had to happen before this departure could take place!

First of all, my parents and Aunt Elise, against all expectation, somehow made peace after Tesson's disappearance. Because, instead of breaking off relations, as would seem reasonable between people who had until then disliked each other and were no longer united in any way, they drew closer. Several times, my father went to Rue du Chapître by himself, and my mother knew it, because I heard her asking:

"Is her sister still with her?"

And yet, while Tesson was alive, my mother had been jealous of Aunt Elise.

To allow me to leave home, other unexpected changes had to happen.

Might we not have expected that Elise, free at last, would take advantage of her new situation and make a different sort of life for herself? Hadn't she married my uncle for his money, and now, at the age of thirty-two, wasn't she going to hurry up and spend it?

Before, people had said:

"She didn't marry an old fellow like that for nothing, or agree to spend years in that gloomy house!"

Of course, it wasn't all over. I haven't studied the matter closely, but I heard talk of formalities that would take several years before Tesson could officially be declared dead.

In the meantime my aunt enjoyed the income and part of the capital.

And yet, in spite of her sister's presence, it was my parents who became her confidants, and every two or three days the postman brought us a black-bordered letter, covered with her small purple handwriting.

Aunt Elise complained, I heard from Guillaume, that her sister, Eva, was ill-bred and a nuisance, and that because of her, and her dressing gowns and cigarettes, the whole town was gossiping about them.

I don't know how many weeks they lived together in the big house full of objects gradually collected by generations of Tessons.

One day, Eva was bold enough to invite her lover without mentioning it to her sister.

Elise found them both sitting at the table when she got home from church, which she had taken to visiting rather more often than before.

There was a lively scene; rude things were said, and Eva and her lover were shown the door.

Did I feel that I was no longer part of our home, and of the family? In my memory, I can find only grayness, like the memory of the colorless hours spent in a waiting room.

There was a great deal of talk about money. Had there, perhaps, just as often been talk of it before? It's likely enough, given my parents' difficult situation in taking on more than they could afford. But now I listened. The word *money* had a new meaning, and each time I started.

Several times a businessman from Niort came by car, dealing casually with my father and mother, although they put themselves out to be civil. Did they need a new loan?

My mother hadn't changed. She's never changed. A meal was never served five minutes late at home, any more than it is on Rue Championnet. She looked after the cows and the household as usual, and every Saturday at four o'clock the water was heated for our bath; every Sunday morning there was a chicken to roast in the oven.

My father was more colorless, duller. He no longer spoke to my brother and me. He took no notice of us at all. We no longer went to Saint-Jean-d'Angély on Sundays, and from week to week Sunday became increasingly insipid. I was put into my good suit, on principle. But what could I do?

"Go and play outside. . . ."

I would loiter about in front of the house, beside the lane, not daring to get myself dirty. I'd never felt the land to be so useless. The timber supports had stayed in place since the winter, recalling the time when the fields were under water.

From Saturday onward I was scared of Sunday, and of all those hours in which I didn't know what to do. And then one Saturday when I got back from school I found my father sitting in the kitchen, where he never was at our bath time.

It was a special time. The kitchen windows and the door were covered. Since there was no curtain on the door, an old blanket was hung up, because I refused to undress if I could be seen from outside. On the floor, on a cloth, stood the big galvanized tub and the soap, brush, and pumice stone.

On the table were scissors to cut toenails, towels, and clean underwear. There was a washday smell. My brother, Guillaume, had had his bath already, and my mother was brushing his hair, after rubbing it with eau de Cologne.

My father was sitting on a chair, an elbow on the table, and looking at us with what seemed like indifference. It was my mother who started talking, when I was in the bath.

"Now that you're a big boy, it's time to think of your studies. . . . Don't sit on the floor, Guillaume. You'll get dirty again."

And my mother, who had kept the habit of washing us, rubbed my face with soap and put some up my nostrils.

"At Saint-Jean-d'Angély, there are better schools than here in the country, and Aunt Elise is anxious to look after you."

I was in the hot, bluish water, and let her go on; my eyes were shut, my nerves on edge.

"Tomorrow, we'll take you to Saint-Jean, and we'll come to see you every week. . . ."

I said nothing. I didn't cry. In spite of the hot water poured over me to rinse off the soap, I was frozen. I saw the fireplace, the stove, with its soup pot, the strip of blanket over the glass windows of the door.

"Aunt Elise is fond of you. . . . She'll look after you. . . ."

Time must have gone by, while my mother dressed me, as though I were still a baby. Then I heard her saying to my father:

"You see! He didn't even react."

I had my soup, because I know it was lentil soup. But I don't know what came after it. It's true that on Saturday, after our bath, my brother and I had burning cheeks, smarting eyes, and a kind of fever.

We were put to bed. For a long time I heard my mother coming and going, and when I half opened my eyes I saw that she was putting my clothes and underwear into a basket. What struck me most was hearing a cow knock its hoof on the floor of the shed, and the horse pulling on its halter.

The light stayed on very late. I slept. It was nighttime when the lamp was lighted again and I half opened my eyelids.

It was then that I saw my father standing in his nightshirt beside my bed. What feeling urged me not to open my eyes at all, to pretend I was asleep, not to look except through a narrow slit between my lashes?

Since he was in his nightshirt, he must have just got up. It wasn't yet morning, because the window was dark. And it wasn't evening, either, because there was no light elsewhere.

Had he got noiselessly out of bed, for fear of waking my mother? Why have I a feeling that he was afraid I might talk, that he was ready to put his finger to his lips?

He looked at me. I could see his nose in profile, as it was

when he was nailing the padding to the window, but this time its shadow was longer.

I don't know if he put out the light quickly when he saw my face tremble, or if I went to sleep again. When I woke up in the morning, I looked for him unconsciously in the place where he'd been that night.

"Father!" I called.

It was my mother's voice that replied, from her bedroom, where she was dressing for mass.

"What d'you want? Your father's harnessing the mare."

Since I was able to register certain impressions strongly, was I really unaware of them? Was I already cautious?

Guillaume has often said to me, and he could only have been echoing what my mother said to him, because he didn't, you might say, know me:

"You've always been devious."

Why devious? I know what the word means to him. Was I devious? Was there deviousness in the inexpressive gaze I turned on my mother, and in the cold way in which I let her kiss me?

I was reproached for not having wept that Sunday, any more than I had done on Saturday. Did they know why? Do I know myself?

I don't know if I hung my head, but morally I was crushed by the sense of being punished.

That's another dangerous word to write. Because why was I being punished? For something I had done wrong? Because I hadn't said anything? Because I hadn't said to the policeman:

"It wasn't on Wednesday . . ."?

Because I'd never spoken of the cuff and the button with a ruby on it?

Or, on the contrary, because I had closed in on myself, on my own secret, and had looked coldly at my mother?

It was more complex and more childish, and when I grew up—it still surprises me—I could no longer express it. So, in the kind of regret that stifled me, there was room for a sin that was mine alone, for a dirty, vicious memory: the little girl I had watched crouching at the side of the lane.

And also for a terrible lie I told during my second year at school. We were generally sold secondhand books. And so I had a dirty, battered grammar and dreamed of a new one, with a stiff cover and smooth, crackly pages.

One day I said to the teacher, with throbbing temples:

"My mother's asked for you to give me a new grammar."

He gave it to me. This too-beautiful grammar book, which I didn't dare show at home, made me suffer. I was afraid of the time when, at the end of the term, my parents would be sent the bill for what had been supplied to us.

Children are expected to sleep whatever happens, but I spent several sleepless nights before taking a heroic decision, to go to the teacher during our break and stammer:

"My mother told me to give back the grammar. . . ."

He took it. Did he guess the truth? He's almost certainly dead by now, but I remember that sin and that humiliation.

I sat hunched in the trap. Nothing could ever again be changed.

I swear I wasn't angry with anyone.

Once again I was in our trap, but I didn't notice that it

was my brother sitting beside me, and I was so indifferent to my surroundings that I am unable, today, to say whether my sister was there.

Edmée married a pork butcher in La Rochelle. I saw her house one day when I went to operate in that district. The front is of bluish marble. My brother-in-law, whom I never saw, had a house built six kilometers from the town, near Chatelaillon.

He is dead by now. Guillaume maintains that Edmée gets on very well with her chief assistant, who has always been her lover. They've done well. Edmée is plump and pink. She has a daughter studying literature at Bordeaux University.

Edmée and Guillaume write to each other and meet from time to time. Their children haven't been cut off from one another, and they still form what you might call part of the same body.

This morning, my mother was put out because it was I who answered the telephone and she didn't know what to say to me. Didn't she instinctively say "I'll call Jeanne"?

Jeanne, who never saw Arcey and whom I selected from a catalogue!

Guillaume also maintains:

"You were glad enough to leave home."

Because it allowed me to do academic work, whereas Guillaume had to earn his living at sixteen.

Between our legs, and pushing into my calf, was the wicker basket that held my things. If there was sunshine, I didn't see it. The villages stood, you couldn't say why, in the gloomy greenness of the meadows and swamps. . . . Horses staring at God knows what . . . People dressed in black, women walking quickly to church, girls and boys laughing for no reason . . . And so it was the whole way, for miles on end, with an occasional farm like ours, white and isolated, in the dirty greenness, with some oozy manure around it.

At Saint-Jean-d'Angély, the trap stopped outside a bakery. My mother climbed down. She came back with a big package of cakes. The girl who served her, and whom I saw from my seat, across the goods on display, was wearing a starched white apron, like the one my mother must have worn when she worked as a salesgirl at the grocer's.

The gate. The courtyard, still the same, except that the rosebushes were in bloom. But I don't remember their flowers any better than the paving stones or the black earth of the flower beds, than the steps, or the eight glass panes of the door with a lantern above it.

"Come in," said my aunt. "If you knew how pleased this makes me! . . . I'm so much alone."

And holding me by the shoulders, she made me walk ahead of her, with her. She was already taking me over. My mother, honey-sweet, told my brother:

"Wipe your feet properly."

Among other things, she had brought an almond cake, which my aunt loved, and neither of them seemed to remember the apple tart.

That left my father not knowing where to put himself. In that house, he no longer had the same proportions, the same solidity. He seemed clumsy, hesitating between the various straight chairs and armchairs.

"Sit down . . . I'll have a nice cup of tea made for you. . . . When I think that not so long ago my poor Tesson . . ."

My mother, like everyone else, looked at my uncle's armchair in the way that priests bow—with a respect at once familiar and mechanical—every time they pass before the tabernacle.

"I feel so much alone, in this big house."

With complete agreement, they all looked conscientiously at me. Then there was silence, and Aunt Elise sighed.

7

They must have planned everything, whispering between two doors, making signs behind my back, with the clumsy naïveté of adults being mysterious. Anyway, they managed to leave me all by myself in the dining room, at the table, which was still set; and they had been careful to leave a big piece of cream cake on my plate, which I hadn't yet managed to finish.

It was the mare that gave them away, by snorting while she was being harnessed. Aunt Elise was outside, in the darkness with them. I hadn't had time to slide off my chair before the gate shut (it was the first time I'd heard, from indoors, the loud clang of the gate shutting in the evening).

I stayed in my chair, my fingers in the cream. When Aunt Elise came back, I was looking at the varnished pear that hung, at the end of a bell cord, from the lamp. She felt the need to kiss me several times and to say ridiculous things in a phony voice.

"You're a good little man, aren't you? Yes, of course! I

know you are! I know we're going to get on famously, the pair of us. Aren't we, Edouard? I do hope you're not afraid of me? Tell me. You're not, are you?"

She talked and talked, and I gazed at her with dull amazement. Then we went upstairs. To get around this complicated house at night, a house full of corners, unexpected doors, and built-in cupboards, you had to switch on a whole series of lights, which I never managed to understand, particularly since some of the switches were placed too high for me.

"You see, darling? There, that's my room. And here's yours—you see, very close to mine, and I'll leave the door open between the two of us. So you won't feel afraid."

My room must have been in use a long time ago, when plenty of children lived in the house, because apart from the ordinary bed that had been made up for me, it contained two cribs and a cradle, not to mention a large number of hatboxes piled up to the ceiling on top of a wardrobe.

"Would you like me to help you undress?"

"No."

Then, as if I didn't want to appear to give up too easily:

"I haven't got my nightshirt."

She went and brought the basket that held my things, and you could see, from the way she handled my clothes, that she had never had a child.

"Don't you want to make a little weewee?"

"No!"

Not in front of her. That evening, not at all, because when I was alone and needed to, I didn't dare get up.

I didn't cry; I stayed calm and obstinate, my eyes open. I heard my aunt preparing herself for the night, going to bed in the big room, putting out the light. A long time afterward, my heart thudded when I heard her coming cautiously in through the half-open door and, in the darkness, moving toward me, barefoot.

"Are you asleep?" she whispered.

I sniffed, and she became suspicious, put on the light, and bent over my bed.

"Are you crying?"

"No."

"Are you scared? D'you want to come into my bed?"

"No."

I wonder if, that evening, Aunt Elise regretted having taken me in.

As my memories become generally more precise, which they do about that time, they lose much of what I should like to call their "physical presence." The smells and sounds and gleams of sunshine on objects in the house on Rue du Chapître come back to me, certainly, but without that thick, warm substance in which I had been developing at Arcey.

In any case, I never rediscovered that atmosphere, and probably, once outside the nest, no one ever does find it again. Everything later becomes clearer but more immaterial, as in a photograph.

Was I unhappy with Aunt Elise? Was I happy? I don't know. The months and the years are mixed up; it's hard for me to say what happened at the beginning of my stay with her and what happened at the end. Besides, the greater part of my time was spent at school, another part at my homework and lessons, and another copying postcards in watercolors.

What dominates the rest is the memory of a light, inconsistent creature: Aunt Elise came and went like a ghost in the house and in my life. She laughed, she smiled, she became serious or cross, and all the time she seemed somehow ethereal.

Very soon, almost at once, she forgot to treat me as a child, and talked to me as an adult, talked to me for hours; or, rather, I think she was talking to herself in my presence.

"I wonder if we should go on having maids who do nothing all day and pinch things as well. . . . I know the house is big, but if I had the cleaning woman for a couple of hours every morning . . . What do we need, the pair of us? . . . And I send the washing out, too. . . ."

She talked and talked. Although she sat quite still in a straight chair or an armchair, one could feel her spirit fluttering about everywhere without settling down.

"You must eat well. I don't want your mother to say you came to me and got thin, you know. We'll go and weigh you at the pharmacy tomorrow. I want you to have put on four or five pounds by the time your parents come next. . . ."

I didn't analyze it, but I never considered her at all as a grownup. Should I say there was something protective in my attitude?

"What did you eat at home in the evening? Soup?"

"Soup and cheese . . ."

"Did your mother put cream in the soup?"

"That depended . . ."

At my aunt's, things were different. She loved food but only certain dishes—canned lobster, for instance. We ate amazing amounts of cake and, between meals, chocolates and other candy.

"Eat up, Edouard! You didn't get that at home. . . . At your age, you've got to keep up your strength."

She even patted me like a chicken, to assure herself that my arms and shoulders were getting solid.

"When you came here, you were all soft."

At first she sent me to the local school, without giving it much thought, because it was the nearest, and I have an image of an enormous yard with a wire fence around it.

For a month or more I vegetated, larvalike, in my seat, and the teacher, knowing I came from a rural school, didn't bother with me. Soon, though, it was noticed that I always knew my lessons and remembered everything the teacher said.

I have an idea of myself at that time. Several years later, during a vacation at Beuzec-Conq, I met a big red-faced man on the beach who hailed me by my name, and then presented me to his wife when she came out after a swim. It was Bouchard, the son of a shoemaker at Saint-Jean-d'Angély, who had become a garage owner somewhere in Ille-et-Vilaine.

"D'you remember the candy?"

I didn't remember. When it was time for school, my aunt used to cram my pockets with chocolates and candy, especially caramels. Since I was gorged with them, I soon had enough. I didn't know the other children at school, or the games they played during recess. According to Bouchard, I used to wander slowly around the courtyard, all by myself, my big head swaying, and stop in front of a boy as, in the country, I'd stopped in front of a tree or a bird. I seemed to be considering, weighing the pros and cons; and at last I'd step up to him, hold out a candy, and say:

"That's for you."

According to Bouchard, this wasn't in the least an attempt at friendliness or kindness. He said I was serious and solemn, that I seemed to be following some kind of mysterious rite.

By the second year I was one of the best in my class, but not one of those the teachers paid most attention to. There was nothing attractive about me. I worked without enthusiasm, without imagination, like a grind. I remembered things because I remembered everything, without trying.

I even remembered Aunt Elise's strings of sentences, but I'm sure I found them quite unimportant and that they didn't bother me.

Sometimes, on Sundays, my parents came. I wasn't pleased at their visits; I may even have disliked them.

Things were going badly at home, it seemed. My father and mother were worried. Aunt Elise stuffed Guillaume with cakes, then drew him aside to fill up his pockets.

"There. Eat that tomorrow. . . ."

There were again crises. Aunt Elise would sympathize with my mother.

"My poor Françoise," she would sigh, and give her chocolate bars or some old trousers that had belonged to her husband to cut into shorts for Guillaume.

"Yes, go ahead. Take them. . . . They are of no use here."

Then, the following day or later on, she would say to me:

"When your mother comes to see me, it's always to ask for money or to take something along. . . ."

The word *money* kept turning up in her talk. It haunted her. Every evening she made the round of all the doors, locking them and sighing:

"When you've got money, you're never secure."

These words are engraved in my memory like the first lessons you learn by heart at school and can recite fifty years later.

"People are after my money. . . ."

Sometimes, at the end of a meal, with her elbows on the table, she would look at me with clouded eyes:

"You're fond of me, at least, aren't you? You love me for myself and not my money?"

I noticed that after we'd eaten, especially in the evening, she sighed more deeply than ever and was easily moved. A kind of warm steaminess seemed to flow from her body, and it is only now that I understand, remembering the quantity of food we used to eat together, the bottle of wine we emptied completely.

"Drink up! It keeps up your strength. . . ."

She was very keen on keeping up my strength.

"There's no point in telling your mother what we eat. When she asks if I make soup, say yes. You understand?"

My aunt didn't like soup, and liked making it even less, so we gorged ourselves on lobster, canned pâté, ham, cold chicken, and pastries. Our heads were heavy, heavy with wine, our eyes smarted. And my aunt told me about her business as if I were an adult.

"It's terrible for a woman to be left alone at my age. Whom can I trust? Everyone's after my money, and your poor uncle isn't here to advise me any longer. . . ."

At first, she didn't talk much. It was only later that it became an obsession.

"I can't figure out the bills he's left, and if it wasn't for Monsieur Dion, who's ready to help me . . ."

Monsieur Dion covers a period that I estimate to have been about two or three months. As far as I can judge, he was the chief or second clerk at a notary's, but it wasn't on the notary's account that he came around after hours to my aunt's house and tried to sort out her business.

He was a big man with reddish hair and a pockmarked skin, erect and evil-smelling.

"We must eat quickly, because Monsieur Dion's coming this evening."

They worked together in the study and I stayed in the dining room. One evening I thought I heard a noise in the hall. I went to the door and opened it. It was dark, but there was somebody there. Someone coughed.

"Where's the switch?" my aunt murmured.

She found it. She was red in the face. Her skirt didn't hang properly at the back, and for a moment Monsieur Dion wildly turned his back.

It wasn't right after that, but three weeks later, that he stopped coming, quite suddenly.

"I can't trust anyone. Money! Always money! If only my poor Tesson . . ."

And once, when my father had come to see her, alone, in the afternoon, she told me:

"Your mother sends him on purpose when she needs my help!"

I blushed, thinking of Monsieur Dion.

Was it an instinctive attempt to escape? For a long time, with a seriousness and a patience that exist more often than one realizes in children, I'd gone through all the school recesses, from beginning to end, watching the soccer players.

That was the name given to twenty-two boys with a ball who had a corner of the yard reserved for them; and the older pupils' teacher helped with their game, and sometimes joined one side or the other.

I tried hard to hide my longing, which must have been obvious from my attitude. I didn't want to ask anyone the rules, and brooded for hours over particular kicks. I had no friends, and was all alone. Then one day when they were choosing sides and were short a boy, I stepped forward, full of what now seems to me solemnity.

"Me, if you like," I said.

"Can you play?"

"Yes."

I hurled myself into the game as if I were hurling myself into life. It's a memory apart; no words can convey it. I was hot. I breathed heavily, searingly. I ran as hard as I could, and my temples thundered, my eyes shone, my whole being was lighted up until I no longer saw the limits of the game or the yard, only the older children's teacher, who was looking at me and on whom my fate depended, because he would decide whether I could play again or not.

I can still feel the shudders, like the vibrations of a gong, that continued in my whole body when the bell rang.

On the days that followed I played again. On Thursday afternoons I went back to school to play. I knew, I felt, that I was going to be the strongest, the most skillful, that I could already run the fastest, that . . .

Then all of a sudden, one morning, after about a fortnight, when the bell rang I stood rooted, tottering, in the middle of the yard, which was emptying as the boys lined up outside their classrooms. A voice called:

"Malempin!"

I had a nasty taste in my mouth, and everything moved, everything faded. They took me to the principal, and laid me on the floor. A doctor came, and kept saying:

"Now, my dear boy . . ."

Then he talked to the principal. He asked:

"Who is he?"

"He lives with an aunt on Rue du Chapître . . . that woman whose husband vanished."

The doctor took me home. I can see us both walking along the street at a time when I should have been in class.

"You see, my dear boy, you don't want to do everything at once in life."

He rang the bell. My aunt wondered what had happened. He told her, then made me bare my chest and listened through his stethoscope.

"He's a growing boy who's not very strong in his chest. One of these days it would be a good idea to bring him along to me and let me have a better look at his lungs. . . ."

He wrote out a prescription. For a while, I was made to swallow syrupy medicines and go to the doctor, but I don't remember anything else.

Afterward my aunt used to say:

"Now remember what the doctor said: no violent exercise. . . ."

And she stuffed me with food more than ever, to the point where I felt dizzy when I sat down by the stove after dinner.

I often woke up in the night hearing the sound of footsteps, and at first this frightened me. When I called out, my aunt would light the lamp and say:

"Did you hear something? Downstairs in the study? It's not the first time it's happened. . . ."

Since she was frightened, she took shelter with me, sometimes sitting beside my bed for a long time with her shawl around her shoulders.

It was years and years—and, what's more, I was studying medicine—before a short sentence of hers appeared to me to be a kind of diagnosis:

"Your poor uncle knew too much, you see."

I was convinced this was true. I wondered what he knew, what terrible secret the cripple had known, but I didn't dare ask my aunt. That was holy ground, forbidden territory.

"It's because he knew too much that they got rid of him. . . ."

Isn't it odd that, although I knew, I allowed myself to be struck by this, and ended up believing in a plot against Tesson?

Sometimes I wonder if, at the beginning, my aunt wasn't playing some kind of game. Yes, I wonder if in the evening, when she'd eaten and drunk copiously, when she was soft and moist and bored with looking at the clock while I was deep in a book, she didn't amuse herself conjuring a weird atmosphere around us.

For instance, she'd say:

"When I turn suddenly toward his armchair, I get the feeling he's there, that he's going to be there, that one day the pair of us will be surprised to see him there, sitting quietly, with his mysterious smile. . . ."

Wasn't I also playing at being afraid? I would gaze at the armchair in the poor light, and shiver, trying hard to see my uncle.

"You don't know what he was like! . . . He wasn't like other people. . . . I would be all alone somewhere in the house . . . and suddenly I'd turn and see him behind me, when I was sure I hadn't seen or heard him come in. . . ."

This was the period of Madame Caramachi. There were several periods: that of Monsieur Dion, with his evening visits and the accounts they plunged into; then that of Madame Grisard, a refined woman, an officer's widow, who came in the afternoons with her knitting. I don't know how long she lasted, but I can see her again and smell cherry brandy and there were always balls of wool and bits of embroidery trailing about.

This friendship ended like all my aunt's friendships.

"What a wicked world it is! All she came for was to find out about my business, and if I'd let her, she'd have poked her nose into my investments."

A few weeks later, it was the turn of Madame Caramachi, an enormous Italian woman with magnificent eyes, who would sit for hours in an armchair talking volubly, not stirring a beringed little finger.

My aunt met her at the grocer's or at the dairy. I don't know what she was doing at Saint-Jean-d'Angély, but she was a woman who'd had troubles. She read the cards. Sometimes she brought a bottle of Asti Spumante.

"She used to be very rich, and had as many as five servants. It's the lawyers who ruined her. . . ."

A word I wasn't going to forget: *lawyers*. For they also were part of the pack of cards.

"The postman . . . A letter . . . The lawyer . . ."

My aunt would wait breathlessly for the next card. This didn't keep her from showing Madame Caramachi the door the following week and accusing her of having tried to steal.

She gave as easily as she took back. The cleaning women, in their first few days, never left the house without having their arms loaded or their aprons full. Later my aunt would say to me:

"Another beggar! She was all smiles, but it was only because she wanted something from me. . . ."

And finally:

"After she'd left, there was a chocolate bar missing from the pantry. I'm sure it was her! After all I've done for her children . . ."

And my aunt would be stricken, indignant. She flew into rages, became vulgar, reproached people with what she'd done for them.

I don't know if it came gradually or if there was an abrupt end, because I remember my parents' visits only as if they were those of strangers. I was no longer interested in my father, angered as I was by a memory, or by my imagination, which saw him in the dark hall in Monsieur Dion's position.

"If you'd stayed with your parents, you'd still be a little peasant. I want you to become somebody. What would you like to become? If I were a man, I'd like to be a notary. Then I'd steal from other people instead of being stolen from by them. When I think how I just don't know anything about my business affairs! They muddle everything up on purpose. They know I'm just a poor woman. . . ."

One day, while we were eating together as usual, with the pear of the bell hanging between us, she said suddenly:

"Tell me, Edouard . . . I know you were little, but did you ever hear the sum Tesson lent your parents mentioned?"

I think I turned very pale. As if I were lying I answered: "No!"

But I wasn't lying. I wasn't even sure that my uncle had lent us money. My parents had never spoken of it in front of me.

What scared me was my aunt, her way of suddenly saying something, of asking a question as if she wasn't an ordinary person, as if she was reading into the past or the future. I mixed everything up, her fears, which she communicated to me, the noises she heard, Tesson, whom she was always expecting to find sitting in his armchair, the people who were angry with my uncle because he knew too much, and Madame Caramachi's cards, with the postman and the lawyer.

"I'm sure," she said peaceably, "that your parents hoodwinked me. That doesn't matter. It's they who'll be caught, because they won't inherit a sou from me. . . ."

Why did she talk of inheriting when she was younger than my father, the same age as my mother?

"Everyone hoodwinks me. They think I don't notice anything, because I'm a nice person. Will you hoodwink me as well?"

"No, Aunt."

"All the same, I'm not going to leave you what I've inherited, because your parents would take advantage of it. D'you see? They think the money's coming to them. They've always looked on me as an outsider and an intriguer, but now that they need money they're all over me. . . . Your mother especially . . . She leads your poor father by the nose."

It scares me to put together, after such a long time, the sentences my aunt poured forth in her slack, vacillating voice, while staring into space with that vague look of hers.

"If your mother wasn't so proud, they'd have sold the farm long ago and rented some smaller place. . . . While Tesson was alive, they thought they'd inherit one day. . . ."

Had she guessed the truth? It's possible, but I realize it didn't matter, that she was unable to stick to any idea for any length of time.

She floated, gentle and vague, stuffed with lobster and sweets, slightly tipsy with wine, and, unwittingly, I must have shared her stupor.

She had a new lawyer, a real notary this time, Maître Gamache, whom she went to see several times a week and whose windows, near the school, had panes of green glass in them.

"I've done something for you. I've put a little something aside for you, so that whatever happens you can go on with your studies. . . ."

Put aside! For about a year, these words hypnotized me. I tried in vain to discover what they meant. I wondered why a little something was put aside for me, and was almost scared of the idea.

"There's no point in talking to your mother about it when she comes. She'd manage to cheat you."

Once Eva came, in a car chauffeured by a young man, who dropped her off, and there was a reconciliation. For two days Eva slept in her sister's bedroom and the smell of her cigarettes hung about the house. Then they quarreled again. I heard Eva scream:

"You're mad, d'you know? If there were any justice, I know where you ought to be at this very moment!"

The door was slammed so violently that one of the panes of glass was smashed to pieces.

It was that year that I went home for a two-week vacation. I hardly remember it. The house was flat, lifeless. My father was always out and when he came back he grumbled over nothing. My mother also seemed different to me, more the way she is today than the mother I'd known. My sister played at being a young lady and made mysteries out of things I didn't understand. Guillaume spent all day in the village. Half the cows had been sold, and the new farm hand was dirtier and ruder than the others.

Are there periods of torpor in childhood? Several times I was near the rubbish heap and took no notice of it. I noticed nothing. I was bored. What struck me most was that there was nowhere in the house where I could settle down with my box of watercolors and the postcards that I copied for days on end.

I saw Jaminet again. I didn't listen to what he said, and today I wonder if it is true, or if it is just an idea of mine, that his daughter, after having her baby, married the son of a local miller.

I don't know if it was at Rogan or Fourras that my Aunt Elise spent that vacation. There was no need for the whole family to take me back to Saint-Jean-d'Angély. My father lifted me up into the trap beside him on market day and there were two bleating sheep behind the seat.

I missed the chance of talking to him, or looking at him. Several times on the way he stopped to have a drink and from time to time he cracked his whip. Could I foresee that this was the last time I would see him alone?

"Come in, Arthur," my aunt said to him.

She kissed me three times, according to the rules, and I was struck by a change in the smell of the house.

"What will you have? A little glass of Cointreau?"

I looked up. My aunt was already busy at the sideboard, taking out the glasses.

"I don't know if you agree with me, but I think Edouard is old enough to go to the lycée. . . ."

An empty space. They talked for a long time, my father and my aunt. Possibly at one time they had been lovers or had wanted to be. There was no longer any question of it. My father was dull and without energy. My aunt occasionally looked at the clock.

"You can reassure your wife, who's always suspicious. I've seen to the whole thing and I've arranged for a little sum . . ."

Did I kiss my father when he left? In the kitchen I found a new maid, called Rosine, who talked to me a great deal. It was she I asked:

"Who's coming?"

"Why?"

"Because the table's set for three."

"Why, Monsieur Reculé, of course!"

My aunt, a little later, explained to me, embarrassed:

"He's a very respectable, very honest man, too honest, really, because if he hadn't always been so, he'd have been more successful. He's looking after my business affairs. He's coming this evening, and next week we'll take you to the lycée. . . ."

When she heard the knock at the front door, she jumped, arranged her hair, glanced at the table.

"I'd like you to be nice to him. . . . He's very fond of you already. . . ."

What was I imagining? I don't know at all, but I was disappointed. I saw a man come in who was just like Monsieur Dion, only dark, a man of about forty, also erect, tough-skinned, with twirled-up mustaches under nostrils full of hair.

"So this is our little friend!" he said to me, shaking my hand vigorously.

Then I saw him bend over, grab my aunt's hand, and press his lips to it.

I was stunned.

8

It began like a mouse's nibbling, all the harder to locate because the balcony window was open and so were the doors in the apartment. I was dressed exactly as I had been the previous day, and was standing in the same place, in the same patch of sunlight, and almost expecting my mother's telephone call. Ever since I was a child I've had this mania for trying to reproduce happy, or merely light-hearted, moments very exactly. Perhaps it's more complex and deeper than that; I may be trying, unconsciously, to create a habit, and, by the repetition of insignificant details, to set up a tradition—I nearly wrote "a familiar past."

Jeanne was busy with the housework, as she had been the day before. We were both fairly happy and actually smiled at each other.

She was the first to realize what had produced the mouselike noise, a letter someone was trying to slide under the door but was finding it hard to do because of the carpet's thickness. Neither of us moved. We looked at the corner of blue paper struggling against resistance, giving way, pulling back, trying again farther left, and at last increasing in size. Then Jeanne picked up the letter, held it out to me, and sighed.

"It's from your brother."

Not acrimoniously, I must admit. A stranger might have thought a letter from my brother was a letter like any other.

"My dear Edouard,

I don't dare come in, because I've got a family of my own, and have no right to expose my kids to infection. But I've *just got* to talk to you. This time, it's *really* serious. I'll wait for you downstairs.

Yours,

Guillaume"

I held the letter out to my wife. At first she said nothing. Resigned, I went to get my hat from the hall stand, and it was only when I was turning the door handle that Jeanne asked:

"Have you got your wallet?"

Exactly the same kind of morning as the day before, the same sunshine, the pools of shadow in the same place, the wine merchant's terrace, which had been sprinkled with water.

I looked both ways. I remember a young man walking along, his jacket on his arm, his shirt making a sharp splash of color.

But it was from the shadows of the wine merchant's shop, as I might have expected, that my brother's voice called to me.

"I'm coming. . . ."

I was annoyed, shocked, I must admit. I knew that place, since it was opposite my home. The owner supplied our wood and coal. His wife had a goiter. There was nothing wrong in . . .

I understand myself. It was barely ten in the morning and Guillaume hastened to gulp down the contents of his glass so that I wouldn't see what was in it; I'd guessed the opaline contents. Not that he was a drunkard. But with five minutes to wait, he needed to go into a small shop like that and have a glass of something. Immediately at home there, he was at once familiar with the owner, male or female, with the customers, whoever they were. . . .

He came out drying his lips and embarrassed, feeling he had to lie:

"I had to make a phone call. . . ."

Then suddenly, with compunction:

"How's the boy?"

"Fine."

"He's all right, I hope? I had the news through Mother. So it was Morin who . . ."

We were walking along, side by side. Still from a sense of duty, Guillaume went on:

"It gave my wife one of her turns. If you hadn't forbidden visits, because of infection . . ."

All this was absolutely untrue, but Guillaume would have thought himself disgraced had he failed to show sympathy. His wife detests us, the whole lot of us, my mother, Jeanne, and me, and by the same token our children. She knows she pushed her way into the family and that we have no wish to meet her.

It is the kind of thing that was bound to happen to

Guillaume. I forget in what town he did his military service; I think it was Valenciennes. In the evenings he used to meet a local girl by the city walls. The girl became pregnant. Her father and brothers, factory workers, came and threatened they'd "get him" if he didn't marry her. I don't know anyone as stubbornly vulgar as that woman, and the children are badly brought up, the household is a mess, the whole place is in an uproar from morning to night.

"What do you want to tell me?"

"Listen, Edouard . . . I think you know me, you know I'm incapable of dirty tricks. . . ."

It had been a long time since I had absorbed sunshine and life as I was now doing along that sidewalk, by that fence where brightly colored advertisements sparkled, and I found it hard to take my brother seriously. Incapable of dirty tricks? Why?

"Go on," I said, rather wearily.

And then added, tactlessly:

"How much?"

"There you are! Always money! You think of that right away. You and your wife, you think of me as a beggar. . . ."

If he'd gone on, he'd have wept. I know him. He gets excited, sentimental, weeps to order, unless it is the apéritifs he drinks that rise to his eyes. And yet he looks like me, though fair, his head balder, his features more indefinite. I am always perturbed when I look at him, and wonder if I'm as weak.

"It's cost me a lot, I swear, to come and see you, and if it wasn't for my children you'd never have heard of me again. . . ."

He looked unkempt. His shoes were scuffed. If I argued with him, he would remind me bitterly that he'd never had my chances, that he'd known poverty with my mother while I was peacefully carrying on with my studies.

For a long time I've tried to help him. Some years ago I got him a job as assistant in a laboratory, but within two weeks he'd become unbearable, complaining that he was treated disdainfully by the chemists, who knew less than he did.

"Hurry up," I said gently.

"Do you have an appointment?"

"No. Just going to the hospital."

I said this merely to avoid walking up and down outside the house.

"I'll come with you. . . . A dreadful thing's happened at the theater. . . . Yesterday, when we were settling accounts with the Society of Authors' representative, we found there was missing some . . ."

He hesitated. He hesitated over the sum. He glanced quickly at me to see how much he could get away with.

". . . two thousand! I'm responsible. If, by twelve o'clock, this amount . . ."

He was already relieved. The hardest part was over for him. Since I hadn't protested, he thought he'd got the two thousand francs, particularly since I was rummaging in my wallet. But all I took out were five notes of a hundred francs.

"That's all I can manage for the moment."

He didn't dare rejoice too openly.

"I'll try to fix things," he said, "get the rest postponed. . . ."

He came a little farther down the street with me.

"Tell me, Guillaume . . ."

"Did . . ."

We had stopped on the edge of the sidewalk to let cars go by, and I made up my mind.

"Nothing!"

"What did you want to ask me? You know, Edouard, you can trust me. I'd lay down my life for you. If you're in any trouble . . ."

"No! Nothing . . ."

All I wanted was to ask him for details about my father's death, about what happened at Arcey at the time. Because I've only the scantiest notion of what my father died of. And I know Monsieur Reculé almost better than the man who gave me life.

Did I start a more personal life at the lycée, where I boarded? Was I just at a vegetative stage? What I know about that time I don't know well; there are gaps, and no doubt distortions as well.

Monsieur Reculé didn't start living with my aunt right away. They both wanted to get married, but came up against difficulties because of Tesson's disappearance. Finally, in spite of her fear of public opinion, she took Monsieur Reculé in as a so-called lodger, and put him officially in a small room on the second floor.

When I spent the night at her house, he did in fact sleep above me, and I can still hear his footsteps on the floor. I wonder, too, why he walked back and forth for more than an hour before going to bed.

One day, my aunt told me very mysteriously:

"You're not going to see us for a few weeks. . . ."

They left together. I got a postcard of the jetty and casino at Nice, all amazing blues and pinks. On the back was written:

"Love from your uncle and aunt."

They were married. Aunt Elise told me so when they got back and Monsieur Reculé was at last installed in the big bed. Almost at once, my aunt appeared nervous and uneasy. She put more powder on her face, but it must have been badly applied because it gave her a moon face. She came to visit me in the school parlor.

"You mustn't tell your uncle you've seen me. . . . Here, put these in your pocket, quick. . . . Don't say anything about it. . . ."

She would hand me some candy or coins, looking over her shoulder, afraid she'd been followed.

"He's not like other people. . . . You'll understand later. . . . When I think of my poor Tesson . . ."

I had nothing specific to reproach my new uncle with. He welcomed me with the seriousness that came naturally to him. But his somber, shining, long-lashed eyes always frightened me, and I now find, God knows why, that he had something about him of the mass murderer Landru.

I have a memory that might clarify things for me, but it is vague, the more so because, being ashamed of it, I have done all I can to forget it. It was of one of my free nights, which I spent at Rue du Chapître, where I still had my room. I had already been asleep, and it must have been the middle of the night. I heard murmurs, noises, and saw a light under the door. I went over to it, glued my eye to the keyhole of their bedroom, and saw my uncle standing in his nightshirt, and my aunt, also in her nightdress.

"Beg my forgiveness, you trollop!" he growled. "I want you to beg my forgiveness. On your knees. Faster than that! Crawl, now!"

I was stunned. I could have sworn that Monsieur Reculé wasn't furious, that he was speaking coldly, in a rather colorless voice.

"I'm sorry. . . . I'm getting down on my knees. . . . I'm just a wretched creature and I deserve to be beaten."

But suddenly he said:

"Didn't you hear something?"

He left my aunt in the middle of the floor and went toward the communicating door, with his twirled-up mustaches making a great black stain in the middle of his face over his nightshirt. I flung myself into bed and covered my head.

My life was no longer there, still less at Arcey. From time to time my mother came to see me, sometimes with my father, and I felt things weren't going well, but made no effort to find out about them.

As for my aunt, she appeared more and more agitated and uneasy. The motion of her eyes upset me. I myself developed a shifty look, because I couldn't forget the scene in the bedroom.

"If you only knew, my poor Edouard! . . . I've paid for my sins. . . . It's sheer hell. . . . That man beats me. . . . One day he'll kill me. . . ."

Then, without any transition, with contained satisfaction:
"He'll see!"

Still the same instability; her thoughts were like birds
perching somewhere, anywhere, but only for a second, then
quickly landing somewhere else and moving on.

"Later, when you're a lawyer, you'll avenge us all. . . .
That reminds me . . . I'd forgotten . . . I've brought you
some candy. . . . Hide it."

Why hide it?

Once, months later, she wept and sniffled, her eyes red
in her swollen face. She might have been a little girl who
had grown too fast, or a monstrous, flabby doll.

"It's terrible, Edouard! . . . If I told what's happened,
no one would believe me. They'd think I was mad."

Then, when I was least expecting it, she suddenly pulled
up her skirts, and showed me her broad white thigh, where
shadows were beginning to show.

"You see? This is where he's beaten me. When I think
how happy we were together, you and I . . ."

I must have been twelve at the time, and was unable to
understand. I was even more surprised, and crushed, too, by
the speed of events. One Thursday, I arrived at Rue du
Chapître. The door wasn't shut. I saw a stranger in the doorway, but took no notice of him. In the hall, at the bottom
of the stairs, Monsieur Reculé was standing in an odd position. He was leaning with both arms against the wall, his
head between them, and his back was shaken by violent
spasms. He was weeping, interrupted by screams.

"Come over here, Edouard. . . ."

It was my mother, who had opened the dining-room door

and drew me into the room. Her eyes were red, too. I caught a glimpse of fat Madame Caramachi drinking a cup of coffee.

Above us, people were walking about, seemingly struggling in my aunt's bedroom.

"Why aren't you at school?" my mother asked, obviously thinking of something else.

"It's Thursday. . . ."

She hadn't shut the door behind us. From the bedroom, the uproar had emerged onto the staircase. The rattling noises in Monsieur Reculé's throat had grown louder, until they sounded like the cries of an animal in the night, in the woods.

I had a confused sight of a woman, my aunt, being led away forcibly by some men, struggling in their arms and trying to grab the wall, the door frames, anything. My mother turned her head away. Madame Caramachi burst into tears.

At last the door slammed. A car that I hadn't noticed when I arrived was moving away. My mother made the sign of the cross and, after hesitating, declared:

"Your poor aunt is mad! She's got to be locked up!"

Monsieur Reculé didn't join us in the dining room. He went and hid himself in some corner of the house.

"You mustn't come here any more," my mother told me. "You mustn't see that man there again. . . . He's no longer your uncle."

We had eaten. In all family tragedies, we ended up eating. Madame Caramachi had stayed on. They'd been careful, but I'd caught snatches of conversation: Monsieur

Reculé had been beating my aunt and had driven her mad with his ill-treatment. I think a complaint had even been lodged with the police, and an investigation started.

Then, several weeks later, I heard that my aunt had died in the asylum. I don't know why I wasn't taken to the funeral. I don't know where Aunt Elise is buried, either.

What is extraordinary is that she had done all she said she'd do. In her will, she left me a sum of money (twenty thousand francs, if I'm not mistaken), exclusively to pay for my education until I was twenty-one. She hated lawyers, so she entrusted the money to the school principal, who was to take care of my board and tuition.

As for the rest of Tesson's fortune, it went to the Society for the Protection of Animals.

There was a long lawsuit. But my poor dead aunt Elise got her own way in the end.

Almost at the same time, the principal had me brought to his study, made me sit down, took on a serious and gentle expression, and gave his words proper emphasis.

"Now that you're a man . . ."

I already knew. I can't say exactly why, but I knew, and looked at him hard-eyed.

"You must be brave, you must think . . ."

I didn't flinch. Staring straight at him, I let him go on to the end. My father had died, quite suddenly, not at home, but at his brother Jaminet's, where he had dropped in for a visit.

"He didn't suffer. He was drinking a glass of wine with friends. . . . He dropped the glass and fell forward, struck . . ."

When I went home and saw him on the bed, I couldn't

kiss him. I was afraid. And, I must admit, in a hurry to get out of the house.

That's why my brother always says:

"You never knew the bad times we had in the family!"

It's true. I didn't want to know them. I know that my mother and brother suffered financial embarrassments, that there were ugly scenes, that my mother several times went to beg the principal to hand over part of the money set aside for me.

They sold everything by auction. It was winter. An even worse period began, one they never talk about in the family, except by hinting at it.

Did my mother really go to work as a servant? Only once, during a row, did Guillaume use the word; as a rule they used the term "housekeeper," and made it appear that she had lived with some old people at Niort, more like a friend.

Later, they had to gather together a tiny sum, twelve hundred francs, and it took them weeks. It was the deposit needed as guaranty for the management of a co-operative.

The business was settled. It was a small country shop at Dompierre, two windows with groceries and seeds, and, inside, rows of casks: red and white wine, kerosene. The door set off a bell when it opened, and my mother appeared from the kitchen, sketching a sad, resigned smile and asking the little girl who had come in with a jug or basket:

"What do you want?"

As for me, they no longer thought of me as part of the

family and I never had a place in that house. I remember it with nothing but discomfort.

This is what matters! I walked the rest of the way unconsciously, and crossed the vestibule, with its everlasting draft. Then I swear I must have given the porter a friendly wave, pushed the glass door, and walked down the long stone-flagged passage.

"Dr. Malempin!" said a pleased, surprised voice.

It was Mademoiselle Berthe, my assistant, all in white and carrying a pen. She wanted to talk to me, to ask questions, but first she had to finish what she was doing. A glance, in the meantime, assured her that I was well, at any rate; that my face bore no bad news.

"Sign here . . ." she said.

In the office, with its light polished woodwork, I found a man and a woman, the woman hatless, thin, ageless, out of shape from six or seven months' pregnancy. She looked around fearfully and kept turning to her husband, one of those peasants come to Paris to work as a laborer.

"Where should I sign?"

The man was mistrustful, peering at me and wondering what my role was. He didn't know how to hold the pen.

"Just my name?"

The woman was carrying a pile of garments and things wrapped in a cloth and I knew what that meant. Through a gap in the cloth, which was knotted at the four corners, I saw some blue silk poking out, and recognized the doll I'd brought one afternoon.

"Is that it?" the man asked, still surly, then pushing the woman toward the door.

I looked questioningly at Mademoiselle Berthe. She understood, knowing I had seen the doll, and nodded. Then she murmured:

"The day before yesterday . . . She hardly suffered. . . . She didn't want to leave her doll. . . . But how are things at home, doctor?"

She was trying to chase away the gloom. For the first time, she hadn't wholly understood. I was thinking of my small patient in bed 11, certainly, but not in the usual way, not in the way Mademoiselle Berthe was thinking. I had just seen her father, and her mother, who was pregnant again, for the umpteenth time. And it was because of that man and that woman . . .

"You know, I'm asking you for news, but I've already had it. I've taken the liberty of telephoning Dr. Morin every day. It seems your son has been putting up a great fight and is now out of danger."

It's odd, for a doctor, to hear himself spoken to the way he speaks to his patients. It was as if she was trying to sweeten everything around me. I was amazed to see flowers on my desk. Of course, they're put there every day, but wasn't it touching that they'd been put there when I wasn't in?

"Do you want to make the round of the wards?"

She had taken one of my white coats from the cupboard, and was shaking out the stiff cloth.

"We've lots of new patients. . . . I must tell Gerbert. . . ."

He was one of the interns. And here we were, the three of us, walking from bed to bed. . . .

Isn't it strange that I got back at my usual hour and that I don't remember taking the elevator, or looking for the key in my pocket? It was a miracle that it was there, because I hadn't planned to go out. I came out of my trance, anyway, at the very moment when I turned the key in the lock, remembering that we were without a maid. I hung up my hat and crossed the hall, then the living room, which during consulting hours was used as a waiting room.

I hadn't made any special effort to walk noiselessly. Was I trying unconsciously to imitate the lightness of the air that day?

I stopped. No one was expecting me. No one knew I was there. Bilot's door was open. While I was out Jeanne had drawn back the curtains. I tiptoed close to look and saw Bilot sitting up in bed, his back propped up by pillows.

They weren't worried about anything. *They* thought themselves alone. Bilot was smiling, and his smile was trustful; he looked as if he were smiling at the angels, and his eyelids were creased in that disarming way which makes it impossible to scold him when he smiles.

There were no more phials on the bedside table. You'd have thought there was no more illness in the room, that it had been swept away like dust or smoke. I needed to take no further step, merely to lean forward to discover another face, Jeanne's.

She creases her eyelids exacly like Bilot!

She was smiling like him. She was smiling as if she were ageless, with a smile of total purity.

I didn't realize right away what they were doing. Then I did. Bilot was moving the fingers of one hand, my wife came close with her mouth, as if to bite them, and he was folding his fingers fearfully. He laughed. She laughed.

They hadn't heard me. They were conscious only of themselves. Bilot was looking at her as if she were the whole world, and God, and himself for good measure, as if she were everything, all security and all joy.

Is it true that I grimaced, that I . . .

Jeanne seized a small finger between her teeth, or, rather, between her lips, and her eyes . . .

Suddenly her eyes changed, the pupils became quite still and lifeless. Everything quieted down. Everything was extinguished. She turned her head and, embarrassed, changed her position.

"You are back," she said.

I coughed and looked elsewhere. I couldn't look in their direction. What I said I don't know, but I did say something, quickly, because I had to speak quickly. I moved some object, and I'm sure I was just going to shut the window, because that would gain time.

And all at once I was frightened, seized with panic, thinking of the notebook I must have left on the table.

Jeanne was standing in front of me.

"Have you been to the hospital?" she asked.

How had she guessed? Why was she glad I'd gone there?

"Yes. Well, as I was nearby . . ."

Had she read it? Had she not read it? I wanted to slip in some question to find out. Instead I asked a silly one:

"Has anyone come?"

I wonder if she didn't guess, if she didn't do it on purpose to reassure me.

"Only Morin. He stayed for over an hour. He was very pleased with the way things have . . ."

Had she noticed that I was staring, that I didn't know

what to do or where to stand, that I didn't dare go into
Bilot's room, as if I was afraid I'd break something in it,
merely by being there?

Was it my fault? What did I know about her?

I've done all I can. For twelve years—what am I talking
about?—for twenty, thirty years I've been walking on tiptoe,
scarcely daring to breathe!

Because I've learned that everything is fragile, everything around us, all we take for reality and life: luck, sense,
peace of mind. . . . And health, too! . . . And honesty . . .

Some days, if I'd let myself go . . .

That's got nothing to do with Tesson, with my father,
my mother, my aunt, with all the Reculés in the world. . . .

I know . . . I feel . . .

And yet I was suffering already to think of Jean at my
mother's, and in a hurry to have him back here, among us.

We must, we simply must, close the circle quickly.

We must walk on tiptoe, carefully.

We must lie low and speak out strongly:

"This belongs to me. . . . This is my home. . . . This
is *me* forever. . . ."

I haven't failed to notice that Jean's sensuality is developing early, with the risk . . .

I must talk to him.

As for my wife, I'll have her X-rayed next week, because
of her ulcer. . . .

As for myself . . . I've often thought of my father's
sudden death. Obviously it must have been . . .

Otherwise everything would be too easy! As on the day
when I thought all that was needed to reach out for sunshine
and the South was to buy a new car and set off.

Did Aunt Elise, who had married her ugly old Tesson for . . .

And my mother who . . .

My father . . .

The sun, coming in obliquely, cut the room in two. My wife dashed out to the kitchen, where a stew was cooking.

All alone in bed, Bilot said:

"What have you brought me?"

And I didn't know what to answer. I was ashamed. I'd taken a doll to my small patient in Number 11.

A reply rose to my lips, but I didn't dare. There was no point in it. It was part of all the rubbish I wanted to be rid of.

"Myself!"

And, jealous of the look he had given his mother and not me, embarrassed by the definite questions conveyed with the pupils of his eyes, I said:

"We're going to spend the summer vacation in the South. . . ."

Stupidly, I touched wood. I told myself I must burn the notebook, and knew that I wouldn't.